STAR WARS®
DARK FORCES™

Rebel Agent

STAR WARS®
DARK FORCES™
Rebel Agent

Written by
WILLIAM C. DIETZ

Illustrated by
EZRA TUCKER

A DARK HORSE COMICS®
& BOULEVARD/PUTNAM BOOK

Dark Horse Comics
Publisher Mike Richardson
10956 SE Main Street
Milwaukie, OR 97222

G. P. Putnam's Sons
Publishers Since 1838
A member of Penguin Putnam Inc.
200 Madison Avenue
New York, NY 10016

Editors
LYNN ADAIR
GINJER BUCHANAN
& ALLAN KAUSCH

Jacket and book designers
JULIE GASSAWAY
& BRIAN GOGOLIN

Rebel Agent calligrapher
ARTHUR BAKER

This trilogy of graphic story albums is based on the characters and situations from LucasArts' DARK FORCES and JEDI KNIGHT games and would not have been possible without the invaluable assistance of Justin Chin and the development staff of LucasArts Entertainment Company.

This is book two of a trilogy:
*Star Wars®: Dark Forces™ — Soldier for the Empire,
Rebel Agent,* and *Jedi Knight.*

Library of Congress Cataloging-in-Publication Data

Dietz, William C.
Star Wars: dark forces, rebel agent / by William C. Dietz.
p. cm.
Sequel to: Star Wars: dark forces, soldier for the empire
ISBN 0-399-14396-3 (alk. paper)
I. Title.
PS3554.I388D3 1998   97-40736
CIP
813'.54—dc21

Printed in Canada
1 3 5 7 9 10 8 6 4 2

>—I‹›—O—‹›I—‹

To Isaac Asimov, John Buchan,
Daniel Defoe, Sir Arthur Conan
Doyle, Alexandre Dumas, C. S. Forester,
Robert A. Heinlein, Aldous Huxley,
Franz Kafka, Rudyard Kipling,
Andre Norton, Douglas Reeman, Robert
Louis Stevenson, Mark Twain,
and so many more.

My thanks to Ezra Tucker for
the art that graces this book; to
Justin Chin and the team that created
DARK FORCES; to the eternally helpful
Lucy Autrey Wilson, Allan Kausch,
David Scroggy, Lynn Adair, and
Ginjer Buchanan; and last, but
certainly not least, to George
Lucas and the other minds who
created this universe. May the
Force be with you.

BILL DIETZ

To my wife Nancy and my
kids Noël and Nelson for their
love and understanding.

Thanks to God, David
Scroggy, and Lucasfilm for
this incredible opportunity.

EZRA TUCKER

>—I‹›—O—‹›I—‹

Rebel Agent

CHAPTER 1

Morgan Katarn was afraid. Afraid that he had missed something important, afraid that the planet which hung just beyond the transparisteel view port would prove unsuitable, and afraid that in spite of his considerable efforts, the Imperials would find the three hundred and forty-seven men, women, and children under his care and transport them to slave labor camps from which few, if any, would return.

All because they had exercised that most basic of human liberties — the right of free speech. First in meetings held within the privacy of their own homes, then in loosely organized gatherings, and finally in Baron's Hed, Sulon's principal city. Because the demonstration was over before Imperial forces had time to react, the colonists escaped without arrest, much to the local Commandant's embarrassment.

However, thanks to the holos that had been taken and a traitor in their midst, it was only a matter of time before the "agitators" would be identified and punished.

Even though Morgan Katarn admired the philosophy of nonviolent resistance, which the demonstrators espoused, and believed the strategy would work in the long run, he feared the "long run" might last a thousand years — a period of time during which millions might suffer and die. That being the case, he had elected to stay home. Some of the demonstrators had labeled him a coward and pointed out that nonviolent resistance often required more courage than combat, but Morgan stuck to his convictions. Armed resistance had weakened the Empire's grip — and armed resistance would bring it down.

The Imperials could have responded to the demonstration in any number of ways — including show trials, transportation to slave labor camps, or out-and-out murder. But the demonstrators considered that unlikely . . . until three families were massacred in one night, their homes burned to the ground, and Imperial AT-AT tracks left for everyone to see.

Morgan Katarn had their attention by then and, with funding supplied by Rebel sympathizers, organized an escape plan. The effort that followed, which involved hiding the fugitives on a long-abandoned space station, hiring a blockade runner, slipping out of Sulon's system undetected, and making the long, uncomfortable flight to Ruusan, had been nothing less than a series of minor miracles. However, the hard part was over now — or so Morgan hoped. He turned to Captain Jerg.

The merchant officer was a tall, somewhat gaunt man, who favored a Republic-era Captain's cap, a sweat-stained tank top, and once-white pants. His feet, for reasons Morgan had never understood, went eternally bare. "So," Morgan asked, "what's it like down there?"

Jerg gave a characteristic shrug. "There's some low-profile indigs, pockets of ruins, and a lot of good-for-nothing real estate. The planet has a class-one atmosphere though, enough gravity to keep your feet on the ground, and something more . . . Something so special you can't hardly find it anymore."

Morgan saw the gleam in the other man's eyes, knew it was a setup, and asked the question anyway. Success, assuming such a thing was possible, would hinge on Jerg's cooperation. "Yes? What's that?"

Jerg grinned. His teeth were badly in need of cleaning. "There ain't no Imperials down there. . . . Get it?"

Morgan forced a chuckle, indicated that he "got it," and posed the obvious question. "So how did you find it? And what's to say the Imperials won't, too?"

Jerg shrugged. "It happened about ten years ago. There was a Destroyer on our tails. We took a random hyperspace jump and wound up here. As for the rest, heck, you're old enough to know there ain't no certainties, no way to be absolutely sure of the crew or to guarantee that an Imperial probe droid won't drop in for a look-see. But it ain't happened yet . . . and that makes this the best shot you're likely to get."

The answer wasn't especially reassuring, but it was honest, and the fact that Jerg and his crew continued to store contraband on Ruusan was a testament to the blockade runner's faith. That, plus the fact that the space station's holds were both cold and crowded helped make the decision. Morgan nodded. "All right, then . . . take them down."

The *Cyclops* carried two shuttles — both of which were kept in excellent repair — a necessity since so many of Jerg's cargoes were transferred under less-than-ideal circumstances. And it was a good thing, since each shuttle would have to make nine trips before the fugitives and their gear arrived dirtside. Morgan accompanied the first load of passengers.

The colonists, for that's what they were about to become, were an uncharacteristically silent group — teeth chattering from days spent in the near-freezing holds and bodies hidden beneath multiple layers of clothes. The children, a normally rambunctious lot, were withdrawn.

Morgan could hardly blame them. Life on Sulon had been hard, but most of the protesters had been second- or even third-generation farmers, which meant the security of a house to live in, whatever possessions they had managed to accumulate, and enough to eat.

Now they faced starting over, and, even worse, on a planet they'd never heard of, with a minimum of supplies and the constant threat of discovery. It was enough to make the most determined optimist a little depressed. A line formed and jerked through the lock as a crew member checked the settlers against the list on his datapad.

Morgan spotted a woman struggling to corral three small boys. Citizen Roskin, if he remembered correctly. The Rebel leader scooped the youngest of the brood into his arms and offered the boy's mother a grandfatherly smile. "Can I give you a hand? My son is grown. But I remember when he was this size."

The woman smiled gratefully, provided her name to the purser, and passed through the lock. Morgan nodded and followed. One vessel was down on the surface, so the hangar bay seemed half empty. The remaining shuttle crouched as if ready for action. The ramp gave slightly as they shuffled aboard. The interior smelled of paint and ozone. Twenty rows of bolt-down seats had been installed in the cargo compartment. A crew woman pointed them toward the rear, and they obeyed. Morgan found a seat for the boy, secured his harness, and did the same for himself.

There was a wait, and the youngster started to fuss. Morgan removed the multi-tool from a belt pouch, popped the power pak into the palm of his hand, and offered the device for inspection. Kyle had given it to him five years before, and the handle bore his initials. The toddler grabbed the tool and shoved one end into his mouth.

Morgan remembered that Kyle had been equally fascinated by his father's tools and, more important, by what they could accomplish. By the time he was a teenager, the lad could disassemble, troubleshoot, and repair anything on the farm, including Wee Gee, the family's one-of-a-kind droid.

The pilot interrupted Morgan's thoughts with a perfunctory safety lecture, lifted the shuttle on its repulsors, and guided the vessel out through widely gaping doors. The cargo compartment had no view ports, so there was nothing to look at.

The boy removed the now-gooey object from his mouth, said something unintelligible, and allowed the tool to slip from his grasp. Morgan strained against his harness and managed to grab the device before it drifted away. His thoughts returned to Kyle.

There were only two things he regretted about his life — his wife's premature death, and the fact that his lack of financial resources had forced Kyle into a choice between life as a subsistence farmer and the Imperial Military Academy on Carida, an institution well known for its engineering curriculum, its unbending discipline, and its ability to produce the kind of fanatics he sought to defeat.

Morgan remembered the day they had parted — how Kyle had looked in his uniform and how difficult it had been to keep his voice steady. "I want you to remember, son, when you're at the Academy, how very proud I am of you."

Kyle nodded, said all the right things, and boarded the first in a series of ships that would carry him to Carida. Time passed, but the questions continued to nag: What would the Imperials make of his son? A man to be proud of? Or a monster capable of murdering people in their beds? And whose fault would that be? Kyle's? Or his?

The boy gurgled, smiled engagingly, and crossed his eyes. Morgan smiled in return. "I don't know about Kyle, but they won't get you."

>—•—>—•—O—•—<—•—<

"Fort Nowhere," as Jerg's crew liked to call it, was shaped like a six-pointed star. All-purpose blaster cannon had been mounted at each of the star's points, the ball turrets ensuring that any attacker, regardless of approach, would enter an effective crossfire.

The cannons, plus subsurface missile batteries and rammed-earth walls, made the fort impregnable by anything less than a full-scale Imperial raid. A more-than-sufficient deterrent to pirates and the rarely seen natives.

A series of interconnected caverns were used to warehouse Jerg's cargoes and the supplies required to maintain the 'Clops.

The pilot produced the necessary codes, received clearance, and lowered the shuttle onto a sun-faded X.

The ramp touched duracrete, a light appeared, harnesses were released, and the passengers were allowed to disembark. Many

appeared dazed as they left the ship, staggered under the weight of the noonday sun, and shucked layer after layer of clothes.

Morgan followed them off the ship, located those he had identified as having leadership potential, and led them through a blastproof gate. The land looked tough, as if it had been half-cooked and then left out to dry under the sun.

Mountains were a barely seen presence to the west. A roadbed so old that only its vegetation-clad symmetry served to give it away angled to meet them. The settlers eyed the harsh landscape, squinted into the sun, and kept their thoughts to themselves as they climbed a hill. Fresh crawler tracks led the way.

The supplies were stacked as Morgan had requested, within eyesight of the fort but beyond the scope of its direct influence, a necessity if the newcomers were to establish their independence and protect their children from the seamier aspects of fortress life.

The site occupied a rise and looked out onto one of the planet's many reddish-orange wastelands. The location, plus the supplies, and the cool, clean water that gushed from the recently drilled well, were sufficient to raise the colonists' spirits. Jokes were told and discussions begun. Twenty minutes later, the newly landed colonists were hard at work revising Morgan's plans, arguing over how to divide the surrounding land, and jockeying for power within a government they hadn't formed yet. Morgan smiled. Things were on the right track.

Morgan stayed with the settlers for three local days, welcomed successive waves of colonists, ensured fair treatment of the newcomers by the "firsties," helped erect temporary shelters, and guided groups into the caverns where mirrors and fiber-optic cable would be used to pipe sunlight down from the surface. Morgan was a farmer himself, and when he explained how sunlight could be combined with fertilizer and drip-style irrigation to produce healthy crops, they believed him.

Finally, when it became apparent that some of the colonists had become *too* dependent on his leadership and others chafed under the restrictions it imposed, Morgan knew that it was time to leave them for a while.

He borrowed a skimmer. It was more than ten years old, dented from hard use, and nearly stripped of its yellow paint. The name *Old Codger* had been hand lettered onto the floater's bow, and that seemed to tell the story. But appearances can be deceiving. Morgan conducted his own inspection and found that the skimmer, like all of Jerg's equipment, was in excellent repair.

The rear seats had been removed to make room for cargo, so Morgan had plenty of space to stash his borrowed camping gear, a crate full of parts, the tools required to install them, and four five-liter containers of water. This would be more than enough if he was careful.

The natives weren't supposed to be hostile, but Morgan took a blast rifle just to be safe, along with a comm set and survival gear.

Morgan knew that as in most desert environments, the best time to travel was at night. But he wanted to see the countryside. By traveling in the morning and evening, he hoped to avoid the worst part of the heat and still see the sights.

He left so early in the morning that the stars were out, and the sentry shook his head in amazement. He figured that anyone who ventured into the badlands, and didn't have to, was out of his mind.

Morgan, who hadn't taken anything like a vacation in more than fifteen years, gloried in his freedom. The speeder hummed, the stars wheeled, and the wind caressed his face. It was fresh and carried the scent of the low-growing bushes — from which aromatic oil could be extracted if the colonists cared to give it a try — that covered much of the land.

For lack of a better destination, Morgan chose to follow the old roadbed. It took considerable resources to build such a highway. . . . So where would it lead? To a city? Full of ancient ruins? He hoped so.

Jerg's crew, none of whom looked forward to rotations on Ruusan, did what they were required to do but ventured no farther than was absolutely necessary. The initial survey, conducted years before, had revealed one low-profile sentient life form, and that was all they needed or wanted to know.

Morgan, who never tired of learning, reveled in the opportunity to explore and observe. The landscape assumed a soft, almost surreal quality as the early morning light painted it in shades of lavender and gold. The air, which was so completely different from the stale, recycled stuff available aboard ship, was fresh and cool.

The feeling of intoxication was so strong that he laughed out loud, opened the throttle, and cheered as the skimmer surged ahead. It was good to be alive!

Hours passed, the sun hung high in the sky, and Morgan looked for a place to stop. He was hungry and, more important, very, very warm. A semirigid awning had been included in his equipment, and it was time to deploy it.

Morgan scanned the terrain ahead, spotted an interesting rock formation, and angled off to meet it. The boulder, for that was what it appeared to be, looked like a half-buried loaf of bread. The sun was just past its zenith, which meant that "big loaf" threw some shade to the east. Morgan steered the speeder into the rock's protection and felt the temperature drop.

Work had always come before play in Morgan's life, and some habits are hard to break. He instructed the on-board computer to run a routine diagnostics check on the floater's power plant and tugged, snapped, and swore the awning into place. It was then, and only then, that he took time for lunch.

The cooler, which had its own power source, was extremely efficient. The beer was cold, the locally grown fruit juicy, and the sandwich filling.

Having eaten his fill and restowed his gear, Morgan decided to circle the rock. The landmark was so prominent and so close to the road that it was certain to have been noticed. Maybe, just maybe, he'd find something of interest.

Gravel crunched under his boots, an insect buzzed in his face, and beads of sweat dotted Morgan's forehead. A wave of hot, sultry air swept in from the plains, ruffled the low-growing bushes, and lost its will to live.

Fissures appeared in the rock. Some were large enough to stick his hand into, though he didn't. Patches of lichen clung here and there, and an animal scurried into its burrow. Interesting but not what he had hoped for. No graffiti, no pictographs, and no tool marks.

Finally, having circumnavigated three-quarters of the rock and concluding that it had no secrets to conceal, Morgan found the very thing he'd been looking for — signs of life.

The first thing he noticed was that while the blue-green ground cover grew fairly evenly everywhere else, this patch of earth was bare. So bare, and covered with strange, striated tracks, that he concluded it was subject to ongoing use.

Of equal interest was the fact that twenty-five or thirty holes had been excavated in the area. All were shallow, and some contained scraps of semitransparent tissue that produced an unpleasant odor and dwindled in size as insects carved the treasure into bug-sized servings and carried them away. What was the stuff, anyway? And, more important, what created it? And why?

At first, Morgan thought the holes were too symmetrical to be the work of animals, but that was before he remembered the nearly identical nests that Sulon's flatwings liked to construct and realized his assumption was wrong. He had no reason to believe that sentients were associated with the holes, but that was the way it *felt*. Such feelings Morgan had fought to suppress his entire adult life.

Morgan had always been aware of the Force. As a child, with no one to guide his actions, he had used his abilities to animate toys, to entertain his baby sister, to nudge people in the direction he wanted them to go and, finally, in an act that changed the rest of his life, to push a bully off balance. Not much, just a little, so his first blow would be more effective. And the stratagem had worked. How could Morgan know that the bully would stagger backward? Would trip over a root? Would fall ten meters to the rocks below? Would die as a result?

No one knew what had actually taken place that day, and no one ever would, except for Morgan. And what he knew, or *thought* he knew, was that he was too weak, too flawed to be trusted with such an ability, a talent that never ceased to plague him, to convey information he didn't want to receive, to remind him of that terrible day.

Suddenly paranoid, Morgan looked up and scanned the horizon. The desert shimmered and, with the exception of a single wind rider, was empty of life. Or so it appeared. But the Force said otherwise.

Morgan returned to his skimmer, his steps not quite as deliberate as he would have liked them to be, and was pleased to see everything just as he'd left it. The decision to abandon the original plan and travel during the worst part of the day suddenly seemed natural.

The next few hours were as unpleasant as the first few had been pleasant. In following the roadbed, Morgan was forced to face the sun. The goggles helped but failed to eliminate the glare. The sun screen provided shade but couldn't counter the heat.

Still, time passed, and the kilometers unwound. Sunset found Morgan at the point where the desert gathered itself into dunes. The road had disappeared by then, lost below tons of drifting sand. Morgan steered the floater between a pair of wind-sculpted mounds, found a U-shaped harbor, and brought the vehicle to a stop.

The Rebel knew there might be, and probably were, better camping sites back in the foothills, but finding them in the dark would be difficult if not impossible, and he was tired.

It took the better part of an hour to secure the skimmer and find the equipment he needed. Dinner consisted of stew and an ice-cold beer. It was refreshing, but the temperature dropped while he was drinking it, and that caused him to shiver. He donned a jacket, emptied the can, and started some tea.

The sun disappeared behind a mountainous dune while Morgan washed his dishes and laid out the makings for breakfast. He found the utility lamps, connected them to the skimmer's distribution panel, and flipped a switch. The darkness took a sudden jump backward.

The wind shifted and blew from the north. Morgan shivered, shoved his hands into his pockets, and *felt* something approach.

Under normal circumstances, he would have refused the Force. But this was different. He was alone, a long way from help, and extremely vulnerable. The talent and the information it provided were suddenly welcome.

The Rebel tried to appear casual as he strolled over to the *Codger*, killed the work lights, and grabbed the blast rifle. The metal felt cool and reassuring as the human fumbled for a glow rod and moved away. Intruders, if there were any, would approach the vehicle, and he had no intention of being there when they arrived.

Sand shifted under Morgan's boots as he climbed the side of the dune. Perhaps he'd be able to see who or what the creature or creatures were from a higher vantage point.

Ruusan had three small moonlets, which Jerg's crew referred to as "the triplets." The first satellite popped over the eastern horizon as Morgan arrived on the dune's wind-sculpted summit. The breeze made his collar flap.

The moonlight cast a surreal glow over the desert, and Morgan used it to reconnoiter. Something, or an entire group of somethings, had entered the area. He couldn't see them, but he *knew* they were there.

Then, just as a second moon joined the first, he saw what he had come for. The natives were shaped like medicine balls. There were fifty or sixty of them, all told, rolling before the wind, headed his way.

The very idea was threatening. Morgan raised the blast rifle, sighted on the lead organism, and knew he couldn't fire, not without provocation. He lowered the weapon, felt for the electrobinoculars, and switched them on. Though larger, the creatures appeared as little more than green blobs when viewed on infrared.

The third moon appeared, adding even more light to the scene. Now Morgan realized the natives were possessed of specialized flaps of skin that acted as vanes. The natives could navigate in whatever direction they chose by raising, lowering, or turning their flaps.

The indigs, for he had no other name for them, had a ghostly quality. They ran before the wind and tacked as a group. They sought out minor obstacles such as boulders, hit them in a manner that threw their bodies high into the air, and tried to float as far as they could.

Something about the manner in which they moved communicated such freedom that Morgan wished he could be among them, rolling through the night, bouncing with joy.

It was that behavior more than anything else that caused Morgan to smile and sling the blast rifle over his shoulder. He was halfway down the dune before the risks associated with such a course of action occurred to him.

The bouncers, for that name seemed more fitting, deployed wind vanes, wheeled to the right, and rolled toward the dune. By the time

Morgan reached the bottom, the natives were a hundred meters away and starting to slow.

Morgan wasn't clear on the dynamics of the process but watched in mute fascination as tentacles appeared from within, curved back over globe-shaped bodies, and writhed when they touched the ground. Morgan theorized that the subtle manipulation of the tentacles, plus friction with the sand, allowed them to brake.

The ball-shaped beings coasted to a halt, stood on gathered tentacles, and opened their enormous, light-gathering eyes. It was then, as the Rebel looked into their immense pupils, that he realized the creatures were nocturnal. One of the natives "walked" forward on its tentacles, made a series of whistling noises, and waited for a response.

Morgan shrugged helplessly. "Sorry, folks, I don't understand."

A second globe approached, used one tentacle to smooth the sand and another to write with. Morgan was pleasantly surprised. The syntax was strange, the words archaic but understandable nonetheless. He translated as they appeared. "Finally, you have come." Morgan scanned the text again. The words seemed to suggest that the bouncers had been expecting him. But that was impossible. He held the glow rod in his left hand and used the multi-tool as a stylus. "You were expecting me?"

The native read the words, smoothed them away, and wrote his reply. "'And a Knight shall come, a battle will be fought, and the prisoners go free'. So saith the poem of ages."

Morgan frowned. It seemed the natives had mistaken him for a character mentioned in the poem of ages — whatever that might be. He chose his words with care. "Forgive me . . . but you are mistaken. I am not now, nor have I ever been, a Jedi Knight."

This declaration seemed to stump the bouncer, but only momentarily. There was a great deal of whistling and warbling as he, she, or it consulted the other members of the tribe. Then, with a great sense of dignity, the native wrote his reply. "An alien knight will arrive from the east. He will fly through the air, stay the night in the city of Olmondo, and request directions to the Valley. So it is written. Knights can manipulate the Force; you manipulate the Force, so you are a Knight."

Morgan felt a sense of wonder. Could the bouncers manipulate the Force? He doubted that was the case, but it seemed clear that at least some of them could *feel* it, which explained how they had managed to locate him. Morgan swept the words away. New ones replaced them. "It's true that I have the ability to detect fluctuations in the Force and that I flew across the desert, but the similarity ends there. Please allow me to point out that I didn't stay in the city of Olmondo. Nor have I asked for any directions."

The bouncer read the words, exchanged whistles with its companions, and wrote one word: "Wait."

Morgan watched in amazement as bouncers danced every which way, formed a circle, and started to dig. Half of their tentacles ended in delta-shaped appendages which acted as small but efficient shovels. Sand flew, and a crater appeared.

Then, just as Morgan was about to ask what they were doing, the activity stopped. A bouncer nudged the human from behind; he stumbled and paused in front of the newly formed depression. His light wobbled over the ground, slipped into the crater, and settled on something completely unexpected — the top of a stone obelisk. It was black, and alien script descended into the sand.

The bouncer's leader, assuming that was what he was, wrote with one tentacle and pointed with another, not in the direction of the recently uncovered artifact, but straight downward. "Olmondo."

Morgan felt ice water trickle through his veins. Olmondo! A city was buried beneath his feet! Who knew how tall the obelisk was? Twenty? Twenty-five meters? How the bouncers knew where to dig was a complete mystery, as was the extent to which his actions were aligned with the poem. Was the whole thing coincidence or something more? What if the bully had lived? What if Morgan had learned to use his talent, had studied under a Master, had earned a Knighthood? Would fate have drawn him here, to complete a mission laid down hundreds of years before? There was no way to be certain.

The question sounded innocent enough but raised the very real possibility that the bouncer was making fun of him: "Are you ready for the directions?"

>—⊷—⊙—⊷—⪤

Morgan rose early, prepared a Spartan breakfast, and went looking for the natives. While the human's instincts had driven him to find safety among the dunes, the bouncers had preferred to spend the night out on the plains.

He rounded the same dune he had climbed the night before, fully expecting to see the bouncers nestled into the sand but was doomed to disappointment. Rather than the bouncers themselves, he found a series of shallow depressions, each covered by what looked like a carefully shaped, plastic tent which was actually made of thin, semitransparent tissue, the same sort of stuff he'd seen next to the bread-loaf-shaped rock. Unlike most tents, each of these contained a strange, inverted cone.

A closer inspection showed that the early morning sun had already warmed the air inside the tents to the point where water droplets had started to form on the inner surface of the cones. Morgan could see that as the water globules grew larger, they would eventually slide down the super-slick surface into the tissue-lined reservoir at the bottom of the depression. Later, when the bouncers emerged from whatever hiding place they had retreated into, a supply of water would be ready and waiting for them.

The solar still in the skimmer's survival kit operated on the same principle. It was an interesting example of the manner in which environment can shape evolution. The human was careful to leave the depressions undisturbed.

Morgan scanned the entire area but was unable to find any trace of the black obelisk. The bouncers had reburied the monument rather than risk discovery. The human felt honored by the extent of their trust and wished he'd been able to spend more time with them.

As on the day before, the morning hours were quite enjoyable. The air was cool and crisp, and his spirits were high. The path, memorized from directions received the night before, carried Morgan into the foothills. The land appeared untouched at first, consisting as it did of rocky, scree-covered hillsides; hard, flat-topped mesas; and deep, flood-carved canyons.

But as time passed, and Morgan's eyes grew accustomed to his surroundings, he saw hints of the distant past. Or did he? Had nature carved out the seemingly uniform terraces that interrupted a distant hillside? Could that pile of boulders have been part of a building once? Was he tracing the course of a riverbed or an ancient thoroughfare? There was no way to be sure.

One thing was certain, however. As the sun rose, and Morgan made his way even deeper into what he had come to think of as "the badlands," the Force thickened and acquired substance.

With it came the weight of his own doubts, failures, and inadequacies. Did he believe in destiny? And was this particular destiny his?

The possibility that it might be filled Morgan with regret. What had the poem said? "And a Knight shall come, a battle will be fought, and the prisoners go free?" What battle? What prisoners? Was the poem little more than historical gibberish, or was it something important, something he should have prepared for. . . . The human hoped for the first — but feared the second.

The hours passed, an ancient roadbed appeared, and he followed it upward. The air, which should have grown progressively thinner with increasing altitude, became thicker instead — *so* thick that the human found it difficult to breathe and wondered why the skimmer was unimpaired. He checked his indicators and checked them again. All were green.

Then, as the road took a turn to the right and passed between piles of rubble, he felt something tickle the back of his mind.

The touch was feather light initially but evolved into a steady hum. The vibration increased until his flesh tingled and his teeth started to chatter.

Morgan wanted to turn back, wanted to run, and knew that was the way he was *supposed* to feel. Someone, or something, didn't like visitors and knew how to keep them away.

The worst part was the knowledge that while he had the natural, inborn talent necessary to handle the situation, it wasn't enough. He lacked the knowledge and experience necessary to make use of the talent. That being the case, Morgan could do little more than observe and pass his observations on to someone else.

The road gave way to an open area guarded by towering rock formations that looked like sentinels. Curiosity plus a sense of personal connection drew him on. The skimmer slowed and coasted to a stop.

Morgan saw an opening, its edges ragged with broken rock, and *knew* the mystery lay below.

The human left the skimmer and started for the hole. The atmosphere thickened, turned to quicksand, and pulled at his legs. Voices, so distant that the words merged into a single moan, caused his head to throb.

The opening, created when the roof of a cavern had collapsed, was a half-kilometer across. A single shaft of light found the bottom, and shadows hid the rest.

The stairs were covered with debris but were still navigable. They curved to the right. The voices continued to moan, and some grew more distinct than others. They pushed, prodded, and pulled at his consciousness. These were the prisoners of the poem, the entities he'd been sent to rescue but lacked the resources to help.

Finally, having curved halfway around the vertical shaft, the stairs came to an end. Morgan stepped out onto the Valley floor, moved under an entrancelike arch, and was stunned by what he saw.

A shaft of sunlight slanted down to illuminate the Valley's floor and the hundreds upon hundreds of monuments that covered it. Some were little more than upright slabs, made from rock that had been part of the chamber's ceiling. Others were more elaborate, ranging from blocky tombs to beautifully sculpted statues, miniature temples, and spires covered with alien hieroglyphics.

The human knew without being told that this was a place of death, a prison full of unreleased spirits, and a repository of unthinkable power. Power so vast, so terrible, that it could extinguish a sun, plunge an entire solar system into darkness, and condemn billions to death. But only if it fell into the wrong hands. . . .

He pulled the multi-tool from its pouch with the intention of scratching a warning into the archway but couldn't control it. The device fell from nerveless fingers and struck the ground.

The moaning grew to a crescendo. Morgan placed his hands over his ears, but the sound originated from within. He back-pedaled, his head splitting with pain, knowing he had failed. All he could do was hope that a *real* Jedi Knight would discover the place, fight the battle that must be fought, and release the prisoners from their bondage.

Tears flowed from Morgan's eyes and wet his beard as he climbed the stairs and made his way to the skimmer. No matter what, he told himself, no matter how many excuses offered themselves to his lips, he couldn't escape the fact that he had failed.

It took hours for the wails to fade, for the atmosphere to release him from its cloying grip, and for the Force to feel as it should.

During the days it took to reach the fort and the weeks that passed during the voyage home, Morgan never forgot the Valley or the spirits trapped there.

So strong were his feelings that the experience was still very much on his mind many months later when his activities on behalf of the Alliance brought Morgan into contact with a Jedi named Rahn.

It had been a long day, and they had finished dinner. Wee Gee removed dishes from the table as a fire crackled in the fireplace and shadows danced across the walls. When the conversation took a philosophical turn and the moment seemed right, Morgan took the plunge.

The words were halting at first, but Rahn was a good listener, and clearly interested . . . so interested that he leaned forward and placed his chin on his fists. Rahn had dark skin, high cheekbones, and extremely white teeth. His eyes sparkled with excitement. "Yes! Go on. The Master Yoda told me about such a place, and I searched for it. What did you find there?"

Morgan finished the story and watched, fascinated, as Rahn paced back and forth. Energy seemed to crackle around him. His robes swirled and were attacked by sparks from the fire. "This is important . . . very important. So important that I must gather a team to investigate. We need experts to probe and understand this place. Then, with you as our guide, we will make the necessary journey."

Morgan remembered the cavern and shuddered at the thought. Still, if it meant freedom for the voices that continued to fill his head, then he would go. "Whatever you say. I'll provide the coordinates."

"No!"

The answer was so vehement that Morgan was taken aback. Rahn saw his confusion and held up a hand. "Sorry, my friend, but the knowledge is safer with you. Much safer. I must travel. And there are those who hope to find me. Hide what you know and leave instructions for someone you trust. Those who follow the dark side would like nothing better than to find this place and use it for evil."

Rahn left the following day, and the Knight who never was etched his secret into stone and left it for his son. Then, like countless farmers before him, he plowed and planted. Winter waited, and people must eat.

He was murdered a few months later.

CHAPTER 2

The planet had been a beautiful place, possessed of long, sunny days, snow-topped mountains, rushing rivers, and broad, fertile valleys. Valleys that had been cleared, farmed, and owned by four generations of settlers.

But that was before the Rebellion, before the resources it had consumed, and before one of the SoroSuub Corporation's mineral reconnaissance droids settled into the middle of Farmer Zytho's Braal field, tested the soil, and literally hit pay dirt.

Little more than three local months had passed before the liners dropped into orbit, and the settlers were "paid" for their farms and shipped to a desert world on the edge of the Rim.

The liners had barely broken orbit when a pair of SoroSuub freighters appeared and sent shuttles down toward the surface. Ten thousand machines rumbled out of their durasteel bellies, established their positions via global positioning satellites, and growled toward preassigned sectors. Each could eat, process, and deliver fifty tons of ore a day. The Emperor would get his weapons — and the share owners would get their money. Nothing else mattered.

This explained why the roads had fallen into disrepair, many of the once-tidy farmhouses had started to sag, and previously green fields had been transformed into machine-carved pits.

None of this held any particular interest for the three Jedi or the troops who accompanied them. Their attention was on the Jedi called Maw. He stood in the first skimmer's bow, nostrils flaring as he sampled the wind, looking like the figurehead on some barbaric ship. The occasional jab of a hand was sufficient to impart his wishes. The helmsman steered accordingly.

The skimmers were perfect for the task. The large, open platforms housed repulsorlift engines and made excellent time over the gently rolling hills. Though vulnerable to ground fire, they afforded clear views of the surrounding territory and, thanks to semirigid awnings, offered protection from the summer sun.

Maw grinned and allowed the wind to support a small portion of his weight. In spite of the fact that the Rebels were clever and skilled at covering their tracks, they couldn't hide what they felt. Their fear sent ripples through the dark side of the Force, ripples Maw would follow inward until that which caused them was located and killed.

Sariss and Yun watched with amusement. Though just as ruthless, they felt somewhat superior and viewed Maw with the same affection that hunters reserve for their trackers.

Sariss was an attractive woman of medium height. She wore her hair boyishly short and, like her mentor, Jerec, always dressed in black. Black, with just a touch of red on her lips, collar, and nails. Her interest in the acquisition and exercise of power made her one of Jerec's most trusted Lieutenants — yet threatened the Dark Jedi as well.

Yun, a Jedi so young he appeared to be barely beyond his teens, sat to her right. She was his mentor and the center of his moral universe. Not only the fact that he had been invited to come but that he was treated as an equal added to his inborn sense of superiority.

A comm unit crackled. An officer touched a button, saw the well-known face, and said, "Yes, sir."

Sariss detected the stiffness in his voice and knew who the caller was. She accepted the hand-held unit and saw that she was correct.

"Jerec. How nice of you to call."

"Have you captured them yet?" The lack of a greeting was intentional — one of the many devices Jerec used to keep others off balance. The Jedi was tall, almost regal in the way he carried himself, and so emaciated that his nearly translucent skin appeared to have been sprayed onto the surface of his skull. A strip of black leather concealed the caves where his eyes had been, and tattoos curved away from his thin-lipped mouth. The *Vengeance* was in orbit above, but her sensors touched the ground.

Sariss smiled thinly. *He* knew that *she* knew that *he* already knew the answer to the question. It, like many of the things that Jerec said, was intended to subjugate her. "No, my lord, but soon."

Jerec smiled. No one but Sariss referred to him as "lord." It was

part of her never-ending attempt to manipulate him, and he enjoyed it. He commanded only the ship beneath his boots, but he needed more. Much more. His words were cold and said more than they were intended to. "Good. I grow tired of waiting."

>—+—•—○—•—+—<

Rahn looked out over the skimmer's blaster-scorched stern. A three-day growth of beard covered his jaw. His once white robe was red with Rebel blood, and black where the blaster bolt had scorched his shoulder. He could *feel* those who followed — and knew what they were.

Rahn turned toward the bow. His companions included Duno Dree, a young and not-so-experienced pilot; Nij Por Ral, a portly professor of ancient linguistics; Cee Norley, a wire-thin weapons expert; and Rolanda Gron, a Klatooinian technologist. They looked for encouragement, and he offered a smile. The wind caught the Jedi's words and hurled them into his face.

"We have a chance . . . *if* we can buy some time, *if* we can reach the ship, *if* we can shake the TIE fighters. Here's my plan. . . . " The Rebels listened and were quick to agree.

>—+—•—○—•—+—<

Such was the confidence of those on board that the Imperial skimmers followed the road at a calm, almost leisurely pace. The Rebels could run, but they couldn't hide. Not with Maw on the job. They approached an intersection. Crudely made markers identified the spot where thirty-six farmers had died in a vain attempt to defend their land. Sariss didn't even notice. Her thoughts were focused on herself — and the task before her.

Maw saw none of the beauty around him. None of the still-unviolated fields, the sun-dappled trees, or the curve of a nearby river. He sensed only fear, which drew him like carrion to blood.

Yun found Maw's talent distasteful, likening his fellow Jedi to a Nek battle dog, sniffing its prey. He preferred more elegant demonstrations of power, such as the way in which the slipstream sought to avoid all contact with his carefully combed hair, or the manner in which a commando struggled to satisfy a nonexistent itch. A rather interesting manipulation in which he had . . .

The missile struck as the second skimmer breasted the rise behind them. Yun missed the actual explosion but turned in time to see wreckage cartwheel through the air and plunge to the ground. The Imperial force had been reduced by fifty percent. The ambush had Rahn written all over it. At least one of his companions had known how to control their fear. He, or she, had gone undetected.

Yun grabbed a rail as the skimmer turned toward the threat. Sariss was on her feet, eyes narrowed, fists clenched.

>─┼─◆>──○──<◆─┼─<

Norley was still watching the effects of her handiwork rain down, still holding the empty missile launcher on her shoulder when the first skimmer started to turn.

The weapons expert dropped the first tube, grabbed a second, and brought it to her shoulder. The skimmer steadied and held. The Rebel's finger sought the firing stud. Something caressed her neck. She shivered and resisted the temptation to check it out.

"Hold . . . hold . . . center on the target." That's what Tech Sergeant Hooly had said over and over again — and that's what she did. The caress felt soft, like the scarves her mother wore. Then it started to tighten, and tighten, and tighten some more.

Norley dropped the launcher, clawed at her throat, and gasped for air. It was too late. Her eyes had started to bulge, and her skin had taken on a bluish tinge by the time the blaster bolt drilled a hole through her chest.

Sariss saw the Rebel fall, snarled an order, and prepared for the turn. The bow came around and the skimmer accelerated. Time had been lost — and gained. A Rebel had been sacrificed. Why? The answer was obvious. The fugitives had a ship. All they needed was enough time to reach it. Sariss snarled at the helmsman. And the seconds ticked away.

>─┼─◆>──○──<◆─┼─<

The ship, the same vessel that brought the team to Dorlo in the first place, was small but adequate to their needs. Precious seconds elapsed as the Rebels ripped the camouflage away, pounded up the ramp, and strapped themselves in.

Duno Dree had dirty-blond hair, freckles that dusted the top of his nose, and peach fuzz on both cheeks. He claimed to be twenty but was actually seventeen. He cut the preflight sequence by fifty percent, eyed indicators as he flipped switches, and wished he was half the pilot he claimed to be. He'd flown his father's in-system freighters for six years. Well — three, given that half his time was spent in school. It wasn't enough.

The trip had seemed like a lark at first, an adventure to tell his children about, not the life-and-death mission it had become. The team had landed on Dorlo in order to convince Nij Por Ral that he should join them. Something he had agreed to do, but with obvious reluctance.

It seemed that SoroSuub's mining droids had uncovered an ancient, three-mile-long wall, and the company had hired the professor to decipher the writing that covered its surface. Not to preserve the remains of a once-great culture but to take advantage of whatever knowledge was at hand. Por Ral had decided to tolerate the endeavor rather than see the artifact destroyed. To leave now, and to do so without securing the company's permission, was to sacrifice all that he had worked for.

Dree flipped the final switch, listened to repulsors scream, and pushed the planet away. He harbored no illusions about what would happen next. It was too late to tell the truth, too late to tell Norley how much he cared about her, and too late to take refuge in his father's business.

The ship came off the ground, spun on its axis, and nosed down the road. Norley was dead, and the Imperials would pay.

Maw spotted the vessel first, roared a challenge, and waved his lightsaber over his head. The ship fired its blaster cannons, carved matching trenches down both sides of the road, and disappeared.

The skimmer bucked as it entered the ship's slipstream, veered off course, and rammed a hand-built stone wall. Maw jumped prior to the impact, Sariss was thrown clear, and Yun bruised a thigh. With the single exception of the helmsman, whom Maw beheaded, casualties were light.

The TIE fighters were waiting at the point where the last vestiges of the planet's atmosphere disappeared and space began. Dree put the ship into a turn, pushed the power plants to max, and entered a carefully prepared trap.

Like all ships of her size, the *Vengeance* mounted multiple tractor-beam projectors. Though normally reserved for docking and maintenance related purposes, they could be used to immobilize any ship foolish

enough to pass within range. The only problem was the fact that they consumed a great deal of power and required skilled operators. The *Vengeance* lacked neither.

Dree swore as his vessel lost forward momentum. He fought to dampen the runaway power plants, and wished he were home with his family. Sensors beeped, a shuttle approached, and he was powerless to stop it.

>-+-◆>-+-O-+-◆>-+-◄

Boc, also known as Boc the Crude, was in an excellent mood. And why not? Life was good. He enjoyed tormenting other living creatures and looked forward to the hours ahead.

A green light appeared as the assault shuttle made lock-to-lock contact with the Rebel ship. Boc released his harness, stood, and made his way forward. He wondered what the Commandos were thinking. The Imperials, ninety-nine percent of whom were human, had a strong xenophobic streak and were suspicious of aliens.

His species, the Twi'leks, had twin appendages that protruded from the back of their heads, which explained why bigots referred to them as "worm heads."

Still, the Commandos were *his*, not the other way around. His to use, abuse, conserve, or spend. He could do anything he wanted with their human bodies, and the thought brought him pleasure as did the opportunity to assert his superiority. "On your feet, scum. There's work to do."

The Jedi led from the front and would have been amazed to know that the Commandos respected, even *liked* him for it. Not that it mattered, since their opinions were of no value whatsoever.

An order went to the Rebels: "Throw down your weapons, open your lock, and surrender. You have sixty seconds to comply."

Sixty seconds passed, and nothing happened. Boc shrugged, motioned toward the hatch, and watched a specially trained team drill a hole through the barrier and shove a nozzle into the newly created opening. The sleep gas made a hissing sound as it entered the Rebel vessel.

Then, with their opponents unconscious, it was a simple matter to force the lock, strap the Rebels to stretchers, and remove them to the shuttle.

The Rebel vessel was left to drift, and the assault shuttle was on final clearance into the Star Destroyer's hangar bay, when the XO authorized a live-fire exercise. Turbolaser Battery Five scored a direct hit. The crew cheered, and the ship ceased to exist.

Rahn opened his eyes and looked up from his position on the deck. Something, he wasn't sure what, looked back. It had two heads — wait a minute — two heads *and* two bodies. One was two meters tall, and the other a good deal smaller — *so* small, that it hung off the larger creature's combat harness. Both carried lightsabers, and that suggested Jedi. The smaller one spoke. "Get up."

Rahn's hand went to the place where his lightsaber would hang. Not the first weapon, the one that he had left for Katarn's son, but the second, which had been Yoda's. The smaller creature, who was known as Pic, smiled. "Thanks for the lightsaber. . . . Hurry up. Or we'll use it on you."

Rahn struggled to his feet. The sleep gas had aftereffects. His head hurt as did the blaster burn. A hatch opened. The giant had an oversized lightsaber. He used it as a pointer. A grunt took the place of words.

Rahn forced a smile. "A creature of few words. How refreshing."

Pic frowned. "Shut up."

Rahn nodded agreeably and stepped out into the corridor. A squad of Commandos stood behind his companions. They were a bedraggled lot, and Gron was bleeding from a recent cut. The Jedi started to say something but stopped when he was shoved from behind.

It was a long march down gleaming corridors, past the sick bay and weapons control center, and onto the bridge. A utility droid crossed in front of them, and crew people passed in the other direction. None of them had the slightest bit of interest in who the prisoners were or what would happen to them. Rahn had never felt so lonely and isolated. More than that — he'd never encountered a concentration of evil like that which lay ahead.

It felt as though the Force had been turned inside out. The dark, inner core was a seductive place in which power could be had, but at the cost of one's spirit.

And there, like a shadow within a shadow, waited the one called Jerec. A man once, but less than that now — or so it seemed to Rahn. The Force churned as the Dark Jedi schemed, hated, wanted, and plotted.

But the good side of the Force was present as well, and Rahn drew on its power, wrapped himself in a cloak of white, and smiled as the darkness retreated before him.

Duno Dree, Nij Por Ral, and Rolanda Gron followed behind, their features downcast, unaware that a battle had begun.

Jerec waited as he had chosen to wait, with his back to the

command pit and his nonexistent eyes on the stars beyond. It was a trick, but an effective one. At least half the crew believed he could see, in spite of the fact that both of his eyes were clearly missing. The manipulation amused the Dark Jedi and fed his gigantic ego.

There was a considerable amount of shouting and stomping as a noncom led the prisoners onto the bridge and rattled off some military nonsense. Regardless of what his position seemed to imply, Jerec had never spent so much as a day in the military. He saw their rituals as boring.

The Jedi waited for the commotion to cease and waited some more. He *wanted* to turn, *wanted* to rip the knowledge from their brains, but refused to submit to such weakness. No, it required discipline to control *his* spirit, as well as those belonging to his subordinates, subordinates who had more power than they knew, or were likely to know, since jealousy, envy, and a nearly universal lust for power kept them apart. That's why he never showed any signs of weakness, never revealed what he really wanted, even when others thought they knew.

Finally, when the self-imposed penance had been paid, Jerec turned. Captain Sysco was waiting. "The prisoners are ready for interrogation, sir."

Jerec nodded. He felt Rahn the way hands feel a fire, as a presence that can warm flesh or burn it beyond all recognition. Even *here*, even *now*, the man was dangerous. Fear trickled through Jerec's veins and made him angry. Others were supposed to react this way, especially when *he* arrived. But him? Never!

Rahn watched the other Jedi's approach. Sadness filled his heart. Here was a spirit so malignant that it rivaled Emperor Palpatine's. If allowed to achieve its goals, it would plunge the civilized worlds into a darkness so complete that a thousand years would pass before the light managed to dawn. The Jedi's head continued to hurt, and his shoulder felt hot. He pushed both sensations aside and waited for the assault.

Six additional Jedi, including Yun, Sariss, Maw, Boc, Gorc, and Pic, emerged from the shadows and added their power to the growing sense of menace. Duno Dree, Nij Por Ral, and Rolanda Gron stirred uneasily.

Jerec, careful to count his steps, stopped five meters short of his subjects and regarded them through long-dead eyes. "Rahn — we meet at last. And who might these sad specimens be? Servants, perhaps?"

"I speak for myself," the Klatooinian technologist growled. "My name is Rolanda Gron, and you will learn nothing from me."

Jerec seemed to consider the technologist's words. He nodded in agreement. "It shall be as you say. Kill him."

Rahn lurched toward Jerec, but hands held him fast. The odd pair known as "the twins" shambled forward. Gorc walked and Pic rode. The Klatooinian tried to back away as the pair approached, but guards held him in place. Gorc activated his club-sized lightsaber and seemed ready to strike when Pic jumped for the technologist's chest. He landed, hissed, and drove a dagger into the scientist's throat.

The Klatooinian looked surprised, felt blood gush through his fingers, and toppled over backward. Pic rode the body down, retrieved his knife, and wiped it on his victim's clothes. His three-toed feet left tracks through the blood. He jumped onto one of Gorc's tree-trunk-sized legs and scrambled upward.

"So," Jerec said reasonably, "now that the stakes are clear, please answer my questions. I have reason to believe that you know about the Valley of the Jedi, that you may have been there. Where is it? Provide the coordinates for the planet, or the location where the coordinates can be found, and die a merciful death. Deny my request, and the suffering will last a long time. The choice is yours."

Rahn had spent a great deal of his life in contemplation. He knew there were things worse than death. "No."

Jerec turned to Yun. "Show us your strength."

Head up, eyes bright, the youngest Jedi stepped forth. His lightsaber crackled into life. Nij Por Ral swayed and fell to his knees. "Please! I beg of you, spare us! Rahn has the information you seek — not I."

Yun, conscious that all eyes were on him, paused, ready to strike. His eyes locked with Rahn's. "So, what will it be old man? The coordinates, or death?"

Rahn, who knew he was executing Por Ral as surely as if he held the lightsaber in his own hand, closed his eyes. "Death."

The linguistics expert screamed as the bar of bright blue energy sank into his shoulder. He screamed again as the blade was withdrawn from his still-smoking flesh. Yun was embarrassed by his failure to make a clean kill. He lifted the weapon over his head and brought it down. This blow was successful.

Jerec spoke as the badly mangled body hit the deck. "Not very pretty. But death rarely is. What of the mercy that men such as yourself prattle about? I fail to see how your methods differ from mine. Give me the coordinates."

Rahn turned to Duno Dree. The young man stood, tears streaming down his cheeks, his body shaking with fear. Rahn knew the boy, knew who he could have been, and found his eyes. "Tell them, Duno — tell them for both of us."

Dree's eyes seemed to grow larger as he turned toward Jerec. The

Dark Jedi couldn't see the boy's face, but he felt the young man's determination and heard his reply. "No."

Boc the Crude accepted the role of executioner this time. Dree closed his eyes. He could hear the shuffling feet and smell the Jedi's breath. Hands blurred, the young man's neck snapped, and he collapsed.

Rahn stumbled forward as he was released. Maw was waiting. The blows came hard and fast, more than he could count, and more than he wanted to know. His knees thumped against steel, and blood splattered onto the highly polished deck. Boots appeared, turned in his direction, and paused. He stared into his own reflection and readied himself for the kick. It never arrived.

Jerec went to one knee and whispered into the other Jedi's ear. The words smelled of mint. "Give me what I ask — or I will take it."

Rahn felt the other man's power and feared that what he said was true. Perhaps Jerec *could* take whatever he wanted, regardless of Rahn's wishes. He preferred death and tried to provoke it. "Why wait? Strike me down!"

Jerec touched Rahn's shoulder as if to comfort him. "In time, old man — when I'm done with you."

Rahn felt something soft wrap itself around his neck. He started to choke and willed himself to die. His eyes sought Yun's, and the other Jedi looked away. Rahn welcomed death's embrace and was more than halfway there when oxygen flooded his lungs.

Jerec stood. A rare smile touched his lips. "Thanks, old man. It might please you to know that Morgan Katarn journeyed here before you, suffered as you have, and took the secret to his grave. However, thanks to the fact that *you* instructed him to leave a record, we know what to look for."

So saying, Jerec turned away. Rahn tapped the energy that flowed around him and sent it forth.

Yun felt his lightsaber fly out of his belt and saw it flash across the intervening space. Warnings were shouted, bodies moved, but the damage was done. Rahn caught the weapon, rose to his feet, and turned it on. The air sizzled as a bar of bright-blue energy appeared over Rahn's shoulder.

Boc came at him, awkward at first, then unexpectedly graceful. He executed a series of diversionary spins, stopped, and slashed at a head that was no longer there.

Rahn ducked, made a sweep at his opponent's legs, and saw blood fly. Boc tried to advance, wondered what was wrong, and fell. Yun pulled him clear. It was later, in the sick bay, that Boc learned a tendon had been severed.

Captain Sysco frowned, drew his sidearm, and was about to fire when Jerec touched his arm. "Thank you, Captain, but no. The practice will do them good."

Sysco wondered if Boc would agree, nodded obediently, and holstered his weapon. "Practice. Yes, sir."

Sariss came next, offered a flurry of classical moves, and was blocked at every turn.

Maw bellowed a warning, charged into the fray, and vanished in a welter of blood. Medics had arrived by this time and dragged his torso clear. His legs, one lying across the other, stayed behind.

Gorc chose that moment to attack from the side. Rahn sensed his presence, turned, and knocked the lightsaber from the other Jedi's hands. Pic hissed and was about to leap the gap when Jerec intervened. A blast of energy threw Rahn backward. He fell, skidded, and attempted to rise.

Energy crackled as a lightsaber came to life. There was something birdlike about Jerec's approach. He raised the weapon and brought it down. Rahn saw an explosion of light, an old friend's face, and relished his freedom.

Jerec looked around as if actually able to see — and killed the power to his lightsaber. The air stank of ozone and blood. "Clean up the mess, set a course for Sulon, and arrange something special for dinner. The Valley is ours." Jerec's heels made a clacking sound as he left the bridge. The rest of the Jedi, those still able to walk, followed him out.

Sysco said "Yes, sir," stepped over Maw's legs, and headed for his cabin. There was a bottle of Bonadan booze stashed in the bottom drawer of his desk. This seemed like a good time to break it open. The bridge crew, their expressions neutral, watched him go. It was a scene they'd never forget.

CHAPTER 3

The Rimmer's Rest was more than a bar — it was an institution, a place where members of every known race could find their favorite intoxicants among the establishment's collection of 1,241 bottles, decanters, tubes, vials, jars, inhalers, and bulbs. And then, with the appropriate stimulant or depressant in hand, claw, or tentacle, members could retire to one of more than a hundred booths, some of which had been engineered to accommodate specific species.

Once ensconced, the average customer would be able to find at least a few samples of his, her, or its native cuisine. That — combined with the establishment's rather lenient policies toward weapons and their use — made the Rest an ideal place to conduct business. *Any* kind of business, ranging from the mundane to the out-and-out illegal, all of which explained why the droid known as 8t88 paused, eyed the alien hieroglyphic over the door, and entered.

Servos whined as the droid paused to get his bearings. He attracted some attention because of both his somewhat antiquated appearance and the fact that he had arrived alone. Where was his owner?

The question was to be expected. But it assumed that all machines were necessarily subordinate to beings having "natural intelligence." An absurd but commonly held notion that 88 resented with every circuit in his body. Originally designed for bookkeeping and other administrative tasks, the first 88 eventually became outmoded and was junked.

Somehow, and the present-day 88 wasn't quite sure what had taken place, his original head and processor had disappeared and had been replaced by a unit that appeared too small for his two-meter frame. Or was it the other way around? There was no way to be sure.

8t88 had only vague memories of his previous existence. Nonetheless, he hated the cavalier manner in which his parts had been reconfigured. With that in processor, 88 was accumulating wealth, a large of amount of wealth, which would be used to find and punish the person or persons responsible for his disfigurement. It was not the sort of thing the average droid worried about, but 88 was anything but average.

No one took issue with the droid's presence, which was hardly surprising in an establishment where the saying "mind your own business" was not a platitude but a strategy for staying alive.

8t88 turned and walked down an aisle. Tiny white lights blinked along the margins. The bar was kept dark to hide the many layers of grime and to protect customers' privacy. Red, blue, and green rings rippled the length of the evenly spaced support columns and were reflected in the ceiling tiles.

8t88 switched to infrared and watched while bodies, weapons, and plates of recently delivered food were transformed into bright green blobs. The man he was looking for, a bounty hunter known as Boba Fett, would be somewhere toward the back, watching those around him, playing out one more day in the never-ending game of eat or be eaten.

8t88 waited for a brightly attired Rybet to pass, and walked down an aisle. The droid's hip made a squeaking sound and drew attention. A multiplicity of eyes checked him against mental lists, scanned him for weapons, and calculated his current market value. Once satisfied, they returned to their own affairs.

Most of the beings around 88 were biologicals or, if possessed of machine parts, mostly biological. 8t88 pitied them. The process of dying had begun the day they'd been born, hatched, or decanted. Yes, science might delay their demise, but entropy would have its inevitable way. Except with machines, which could have themselves rebuilt and thereby live forever. The thought pleased 88 and resulted in what others perceived as a grimace.

The bounty hunter sat in a corner booth, his back to the wall, his jetpack on the seat beside him. A human might have resented the T-shaped visor and the fact that it obscured the bounty hunter's face, but 88 felt no such discomfort. He'd heard humans refer to eyes as "windows to the spirit" but had no idea what they were talking about. His voice was flat and synthesized. "Boba Fett?"

The human nodded. "And you are?"

"A potential client. They call me 8t88."

Fett gestured toward the opposite side of the booth. "Take a load off. Are you representing yourself or someone else?"

"Does it matter?"

The bounty hunter shrugged. "Nope. Just curious. Never worked for a machine before."

With no flesh to soften it, 88's grin took on a threatening quality. "Then get used to it — machines are the future."

"Maybe," Fett replied calmly, "and maybe not."

"A man named Kyle Katarn will enter this bar in an hour or so. He has information that I want."

Boba Fett leaned backward. Light rolled across the surface of his visor. "So? Ask him."

"He may not wish to tell me."

"And that's where I come in?"

"Exactly."

The bounty hunter remained silent for a full thirty seconds. "I don't think so."

"Why not?"

"Because I've heard of Katarn. Some say he's aligned with the Empire, while others claim he works for the Alliance."

"So? You've done work for the Empire."

"True, but the Alliance has been on a roll of late. Who knows? They might come out on top. Either way, I'll sit this one out."

"That's your final word?"

"That's it."

8t88 stood and stepped into the aisle. He was about to leave when Fett cleared his throat. "One more thing . . . "

The droid turned. A ball joint squeaked in protest. "Yes?"

"Get a lube job."

Kyle Katarn tossed his drink back, wiped his mouth with the back of his hand, and triggered the cube. The holo played for what? The fifth time? The man with the beard was his father — and the boy was him. A younger, more innocent him *before* he left for the Imperial Military Academy on Carida, *before* the Imperials murdered his father, *before* the raid on Danuta's research facility. Five years had passed since then — though it seemed like fifty — and the search went on. Who had murdered his father? He, she, or it would pay dearly for the mistake. Maybe this was the night the truth would be known.

The holo flickered. Morgan seemed transparent, but his words were warm and strong: "I want you to remember, son, when you're at the Academy, how very proud I am of you."

Something squeaked as a droid slid into the far side of the booth. The synthesizer sounded flat and unemotional. "How touching."

The holo disappeared. Shadows hid Kyle's eyes. He removed the tiny tracker droid from his pocket, pressed the button on its back, and allowed the device to scuttle away. It sought 88's leg, activated an internal magnet, and went to work. If the larger droid felt anything, he gave no sign of it.

"Don't waste my time, 88. You called this meeting. Who killed my father?"

8t88 switched to infrared, checked to see if the bounty hunters had taken their places and saw they hadn't. Blast the idiots anyway! Boba Fett would have arrived on time. He cursed the human's intransigence. All he could do was stall. "When someone desires information, they come to me."

Kyle brought the pistol up from the darkness. Light rippled along the top surface of the barrel. "And?"

The droid spoke quickly. "Patience. He's a Dark Jedi."

The hand weapon remained as before, only centimeters from 88's scanner plate.

"Jedi?"

"*Dark* Jedi. He is known as Jerec. He has great plans for the rebirth of the Empire."

8t88 saw two green blobs appear in the booth beyond. Help, such as it was, had arrived.

Kyle felt his heart beat a little bit faster. Jerec! The same Jerec who had attended the graduation ceremony at Cliffside? The same Jerec who had sought him out, pinned the medal to his chest, and spoken as if to an old acquaintance?

"*Greetings, Kyle Katarn. You have accomplished a great deal for one so young. Recognition is sweet, is it not? However, remember that recognition is a gift given by those who have power to those who don't. This is but the first step. . . . Climb the ladder swiftly, join those who possess power, and claim what is yours. I will be waiting.*"

Kyle hadn't been aware of it at the time, but his father had been killed weeks before. Was Jerec aware of that? Not only aware of it — but of the reason for it? Had Jerec murdered his father?

The Rebel had no more than framed the question when someone rammed a blaster into the base of his skull. Something or someone laughed, and 88 made a clicking noise. "Ouch! That looks uncomfortable. I'll take the blaster so nobody gets hurt."

Kyle released his grip on the weapon and watched the droid place it on the far side of the table. "Now, where were we? Oh yes, our friend Jerec. He has many plans, Jerec does. Unfortunately, you don't factor into any of them. But I'm not without a heart. Ooops! My mistake . . . I *am* without a heart! Still, I might allow you to live, *if* you answer my questions."

8t88 held up a disk. It was approximately six centimeters in diameter and gleamed in the light. "Look familiar? Well, it should. I found dozens of them in your father's home."

Kyle made a grab for the disk, but hands held him back. The droid didn't seem to notice. "I'm pretty good with codes, but this one eludes me. Perhaps you'd be so kind as to provide some advice. Or shall I allow my friends to indulge the darker aspects of their personalities?"

Kyle eyed the disk and wondered what was on it. "The dark side? I've been there. Do your worst."

8t88 shook his head. "Too bad. What's the saying — 'Like father, like son'? Not a very pleasant thought, given the way your father ended his days. Have a nice evening."

The droid slid sideways, got to his feet, and made for the door. Someone chuckled as another body took the recently vacated seat. It was a Gran, and all three of his stalk-mounted eyes were bloodshot. His voice sounded like a gravel crusher stuck in low gear. "Remember me? It took three months for that blaster burn to heal."

"Can't say that I do," Kyle replied honestly, "but the streets are filled with trash — and it's hard to tell one piece from another."

The Gran was just starting to respond when Kyle reached over his shoulder, grabbed the second bounty hunter, a foul-smelling Rodian, and yanked. The diminutive alien arced through the air and slammed onto the table. The blaster took on a life of its own. It slid across the well-worn surface and into Kyle's hand. The Gran blinked in quick succession. "You'll never leave here alive. Nar Shaddaa will be your grave!"

Kyle grinned. "I'm not interested in leaving. Not till I conclude some business with 8t88. . . . "

The bounty hunters watched the Rebel slide out of the booth, get to his feet, and back away. "Thanks for everything. Let's have lunch sometime."

Nobody laughed.

>⊶⊷⊶O⊶⊷⊶<

Jan Ors guided the *Moldy Crow* down through the upper reaches of the city. There were all sorts of navigational hazards — spires, gantries, platforms, and sky bridges — all of which had been constructed for the convenience of those who owned them, without regard for the public good. It seemed as though an entire constellation of red warning lights floated around her. Not to mention the sometimes deceptive signs that might guide pilots to their destination — or into an isolated cargo bay where they would be murdered and their cargos stolen.

Not that the *Crow* was likely to attract much attention, especially in light of her lowly status and battered appearance. Originally commissioned as a freighter, she had filled many roles since then and had suffered in the process. She was Corellian-built, though — faster than she looked, and armed to the teeth — just right for the sort of jobs the Alliance assigned to its network of agents.

Jan frowned, bit her lower lip, and killed forward motion. The globe-shaped drone-ship rose like a bubble from the bottom of the sea. Repulsors strobed the darkness below as lights circled its vast midsection. Static crackled over the cockpit speakers as the other vessel climbed and cleared the nearby towers. Lightning stabbed a distant tower, causing the view screen to darken.

Jan checked her sensors, peered into the night, and eased the ship forward. The Rebel agent hadn't gone more than a hundred meters before a formation of three ships hurtled past. Turbulence threw the *Crow* sideways, and Jan fought for control. A voice blasted her ears. "This ain't no parking lot. Fly it or park it."

The ships, two TIE fighters and a TIE bomber, were gone before Jan could reply. The Imperials — and there was no shortage — were as arrogant as ever. The Empire might be on the ropes somewhere, but there was no evidence of it in the vertical city. Fighting them, and what they represented, had consumed most of her life, a life that would have come to a premature end on Rebel-occupied asteroid AX-456 had anyone but Cadet Leader Kyle Katarn led the raid to recapture it.

Kyle's act of mercy and their subsequent friendship had formed the basis of a successful partnership, one in which he always found new ways to get into trouble — and she to bail him out. When she was allowed to, that is. . . .

The trip to Nar Shaddaa served as an excellent example. Jan had opposed the idea and believed she had talked Kyle out of it only to discover that he had gone without her. What would she find? Some crusty remains? A full-fledged firefight? Or the little boy "why worry about me?" act? There was no way to know. Kyle was good at any number of things, but teamwork wasn't one of them.

A remote-controlled landing drone appeared, ordered Jan to follow, and drew her toward the public landing platforms. Lights strobed, and she followed it in.

Kyle pulled a small comm set from his hip pocket, put the plug in his ear, and heard a clicking sound. It grew weaker when he turned right and stronger when he angled to the left. 88 and the tracker that had attached itself to his leg were on the move. There was a steady flow of foot traffic, and the Rebel shouldered his way through.

A Twi'lek passed by, his robes shimmering as he argued with an Ithorian herd merchant.

There was no way to know who or what rode in the heavily curtained sedan chair, only that he, she, or it must have been heavy, judging from the construction droids chosen to support the load.

An Imperial officer appeared, his rank hidden beneath a cloak, closely followed by his Commando bodyguards. Kyle felt his stomach muscles tighten and allowed his hand to stray toward the cross-draw holster at his waist. The vertical city recognized no authority save its own, and the Empire wanted him for desertion, treason, murder, and other crimes too numerous to mention.

Kyle bumped into a long-nosed Kubaz, ignored the invective directed at his back, and passed a bank of turbolifts.

The clicking lost some of its urgency. The Rebel did an about-face, forced his way onto an already packed platform, and felt his stomach do a somersault as it surged upward. Where was 88 headed, anyway? There was no way to be sure, but the launch platforms were up above, and that suggested a ship. Once 88 was gone, it would be next to impossible to recover the disk.

The clicking grew louder and settled into an unbroken tone. The droid was close, *very* close, yet beyond his reach. The agent swore under his breath as the platform coasted to a stop and paused while a female Whiphid stumped aboard. Finally, after what seemed like an eternity, the turbolift resumed its journey.

Kyle waited for the words "Launch Deck Three" to appear on the entry arch and jumped when they did. The tracker was so loud that Kyle removed the receiver from his ear. The tiny comlink made an excellent substitute. There was no way to tell if Jan was in the vicinity. But he would hear when and if she called. The Rebel craned his neck, saw his quarry disappear through a circular portal, and hurried to intercept.

8t88 had composed five different lies to account for his failure. Which would Jerec believe? The droid wondered as he stepped through a portal and descended a short flight of stairs. He was forced to pause. The clones were human, wore little more than rags, and

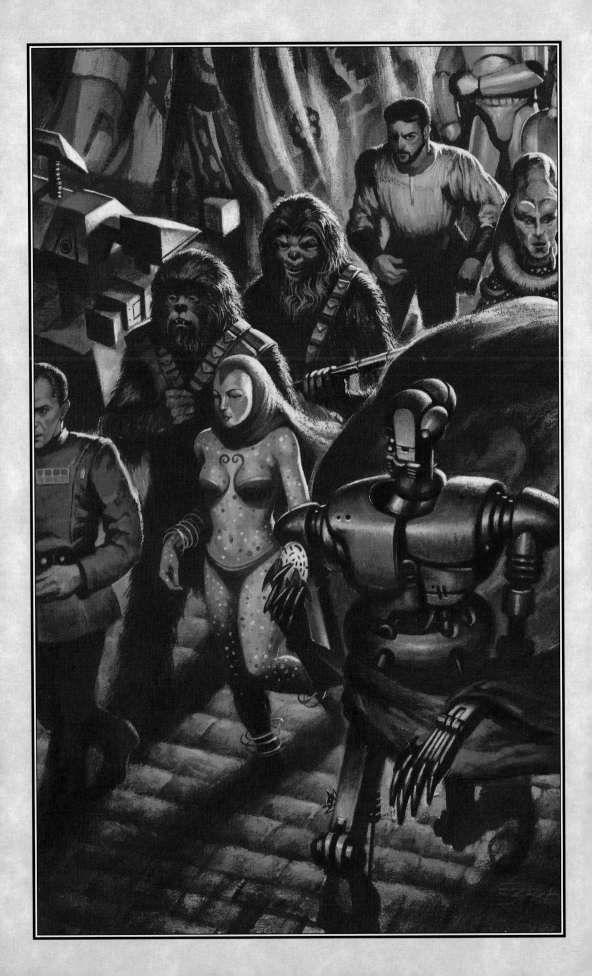

were linked by short lengths of chain. They were miserable creatures with even less freedom than the average droid. A Gamorrean guard issued a steady stream of grunts, snorts, and burping noises. The prisoners kept their eyes on the deck.

While 8t88 waited for the slaves to pass, the brighter of his two bodyguards, a heavily muscled specimen who went by the name of Grentho, saw something and bent to examine it. The tracker clung stubbornly at first, popped free, and tried to escape. The human clamped the scorpion-shaped device between a heavily callused thumb and a nic-i-tain-stained forefinger. "Hey, boss! Look what I found on your leg!"

8t88 recognized the tiny machine instantly, instructed the bodyguard to destroy it, and took a quick look around. Kyle Katarn appeared as if on cue, moving to intercept.

The tracker squealed as Grentho ended its mechanical life. Windblown grit peppered 88's alloy skin. Klaxons sounded as an Imperial shuttle invaded the bay. Like most of his kind, 88 liked precision. The fact that the ship was on schedule pleased him. Various kinds of comm units had been incorporated into the droid's body — and he used one of them to make contact with the pilot. "Punctuality is a virtue, Lieutenant. I shall see that your superiors hear of it. There's no need to land. Just lower the ramp."

The shuttle roared obediently and moved in over the ramp. Kyle drew his weapon, made the leap to the platform below, and yelled over the noise. "What? Leaving so soon?"

Sparks flew as the ramp touched the deck. 8t88 felt a sudden desire to taunt the human. He removed the disk from a storage compartment and waved it over his head. "Is this what you want? Come and get it!"

The bodyguards were reaching for their weapons when Kyle fired. The energy bolt removed 88's arm with almost surgical precision. The droid watched in disbelieving horror as the now-severed limb cartwheeled through the air, spewing hydraulic fluid in every direction, and clanged on the deck.

Kyle watched the arm roll to the edge of the platform, wobble, and disappear. The disk, still contained within the droid's tightly clenched fist, went along for the ride.

8t88 grabbed for his stump, located the arterylike tube, and pinched it off. A stormtrooper appeared, wrapped an arm around 88's midsection, and helped the droid up the ramp. The walkway cleared the platform and started to retract.

An energy bolt blipped past Kyle's shoulder, grazed a passing Weequay, and scorched the bulkhead beyond. The none-too-intelligent creature roared his outrage, swung his pike at a group of Bith sand artists, and triggered a stampede.

Kyle fired in return. Grentho threw his arms out as if to welcome a friend and toppled over backward. Smoke eddied from the hole in his chest.

The second bodyguard fared better at first. She made it onto the ramp and was headed for the lock when a stormtrooper shot her in the face. She tumbled backward, fell off the ramp, and smashed into the platform below.

The shuttle rose on brightly flaring repulsors, turned, and headed away. Kyle took a parting shot, saw movement from the corner of his eye, and dived for cover. He was flying through the air, wishing that the deck was made of something softer than durasteel, when blaster fire scorched the platform behind him. The shuttle was clear, and an Imperial TIE bomber had been dispatched to even the score. The platform smashed into his chest, and he struggled to breathe.

All Kyle could do was watch as the TIE bomber rose — and swiveled in his direction. There was no place to hide. The Rebel stared into the laser cannon and waited for them to blink coherent light. He was still waiting when cannon fire struck the bomber from behind. It staggered and drifted into a wall. The resulting explosion lit the area, triggered various alarms, and activated the tower's emergency response systems.

Wall-mounted nozzles covered the wreckage with foam as rescue, medical, and hazmat droids walked, rolled, and, in one case, slithered to the rescue.

Still another ship descended into view, and Kyle, who was determined to go down fighting, lifted his weapon. He was about to fire when he recognized the ship's beaklike bow. Though not especially pretty, the *Crow* was a welcome sight. Jan was worried, relieved, and angry — all at the same time. "You're always in trouble!"

The Rebel holstered his weapon. "Not after you bail me out."

The pilot grinned in spite of herself. "I saw the vultures gathering over something and figured it might be you. How would you manage without me?"

Kyle scanned the still-smoking debris. "Perish the thought. I wouldn't last long, that's for sure."

Cockpit alarms started to sound, and Jan checked her screens. "More company on the way. Jump on the ramp, and we'll make a run for it."

Kyle shook his head. "Thanks, but no thanks. Meet me at the top! The disk fell off the platform. I'm going after it."

Jan wanted to ask, "What disk?" Wanted to find out what made it so important. But she knew Kyle wouldn't take the time to tell her. Darn him, anyway. He was brave to the point of recklessness and eternally out to prove himself even when the tests were over — first, at the Imperial Military Academy, and later within the Alliance, where his long list of accomplishments was credential enough, or should have been.

All of this and more passed through Jan's mind in the twinkling of an eye. Someday there would be time to talk — but not now. Assuming they lived that long. "Roger that — be careful. I'll see you at the top."

The *Crow* spun on her axis, paused, and moved away.

Kyle scanned his surroundings, spotted a likely looking maintenance ladder, and jogged in its direction. It was a sturdy affair, made of durasteel and welded to an outer wall. On closer examination, Kyle saw that the ladder had been built to accommodate bipeds and, judging from the track mechanism mounted beside it, a highly specialized maintenance droid. What if he got halfway down and the droid arrived?

The Rebel looked up, looked down, and debated what to do. This decision, like so many, was taken from his hands. The stormtroopers double-timed onto the far side of the platform, paused, and waited for orders. The ranking NCO had a parade ground voice and liked to use it. "All right, men — spread out and find him! There's a price on his head — so you could be rich by morning."

The noncom's words were more than sufficient motivation. The stormtroopers had been summoned from nearby nightspots and, though not entirely sober, were adequate for the task at hand.

Kyle took one look, swung over the abyss, and located the first crosspiece with his feet. The rungs were close together — as if to accommodate beings with shorter legs — and ice cold. The Rebel wished he had gloves and pulled his hands into his sleeves, using them for insulation.

The city rose around him as the agent lowered himself into the depths. With a slight turn of his head, Kyle could see all manner of vertical structures, their cylindrical, rectangular, and even trapezoidal shapes connected by sky bridges, causeways, and arches. Everything was so intertwined that Kyle had the impression of multiple trunks all rising from a common set of roots, as if the entire city was part of a single organism on which a wide variety of symbiotes and parasites managed to flourish. And what did that make him, he wondered? A momentary infestation?

The thought amused him. He almost laughed aloud when an unexpected blast threatened to tear him loose. At least it felt like a blast, although there was nothing natural about the behemoth that caused it or about the way the air pummeled Kyle's body.

The ship was far too large for use within the narrow confines of Nar Shaddaa's lower canyons and had been pressed into use without regard for the safety of those who lived in the surrounding towers. A searchlight swept across Kyle's body, paused on the wall beyond, and came back again. A voice was amplified and audible over the ship's repulsors. "Hey, you! The man on the ladder! Hold it right there!"

Kyle ignored the order and increased his rate of descent. A rectangle of white light appeared and was gone. Kyle had the impression of a woman dressed in white, a Mon Calamari officer, and a chrome-plated droid. They all looked surprised, and the woman, if she was typical, frightened.

The people on the ship were annoyed. Cannon fire rippled across the wall beneath Kyle's boots. He had no choice but to climb, even if that meant going to the landing platform above. Or did he? Kyle climbed up to the window, paused, and peered into the room. The occupants had fled.

Whoever commanded the ship took exception to the pause and fired. Kyle scrambled upward, heard the transparisteel windows shatter, and saw lights appear. Stormtroopers? No, a maintenance droid, sent to knock him clear.

The ship, unable to hold its position for more than a few seconds, had fallen two or three stories and was in the process of rising again. Kyle lowered himself downward, eyed the window, and made the sideways leap.

The maneuver was more difficult than he'd thought it would be. His arms hit the windowsill, his legs kicked the wall, and the ship hovered meters away. It was so close that he might have been able to see the crew's faces had he turned to look. What were they doing? Waiting for him to fall?

The droid, well aware of its circumstances, wailed as it roared by. The crash came five seconds later.

The vessel was so huge, so overpowering, that it took every bit of Kyle's courage to throw a leg over the sill, ignore the cuts he had suffered, and pull himself into the recently devastated apartment. The ship addressed him via the loudspeakers. He waved in hopes that they would continue to hold their fire. Debris lay everywhere, holes had been punched through walls, and a fire burned in one corner of the room.

There was nothing graceful about the way he tumbled through the window, scrabbled toward the still-open door, and threw himself through it. He was barely through when the ship fired. The recently vacated apartment seemed to explode.

Kyle made it to his feet, sprinted down the hall, and heard the ship continue to fire. Windows shattered, walls vanished, and kitchens exploded as the Imperials probed the inside of the building. How many had died? The Imperials neither knew nor cared.

The corridor came to an end; the agent slipped into a fire escape and made his way downward. The attack and the noise that accompanied it gradually died away.

It was tempting to take a moment to reflect on what he'd been through, to check whatever wounds he'd sustained, but Kyle knew better than to do so. The Imperials would stop at nothing, and reinforcements were on the way. He took the stairs two at a time.

Kyle considered using the turbolifts after three or four floors but knew they would be dangerous and settled on the stairs, drop tubes, and ladderways instead. And he was not alone. Over time, other beings had been forced into the city's back ways. Now they called them home.

Still, threatening as some of them were, most had no desire to mix it up with the wild-eyed lunatic who came careening out of the dark, blood clotting along one side of his face, clothes hanging in shreds.

They appeared like snapshots, their expressions of fear, hatred, or surprise forever burned into Kyle's memory as they peered out of tunnels, bared their fangs, or jumped out of his way. Gravity and his own inertia pulled him downward.

There wasn't much time to think, to analyze his progress, but certain things were obvious. The city was constructed in layers. By descending into Nar Shaddaa's depths, Kyle was traveling back in time.

The metal beneath his boots took on a different ring as old alloys replaced new.

The ever-present graffiti transitioned from standard to alien hieroglyphics and back again.

Murals spoke through layers of grime, telling stories of a people so wealthy, a culture that held art in such high esteem, that it beautified even the most insignificant of passageways.

Wreckage, including the hull of an ancient spaceship, spoke of hard times, too, when someone or something had been shackled to well-anchored ring bolts and spent days scratching its name into the wall.

The farther Kyle went, the warmer it became — so warm that moisture ran down the walls, rust coated everything in sight, and his clothes hung heavy on his body.

The source of the warmth was no mystery. As Kyle neared the moon's surface, he entered the realm of the city's massive exhaust ports. Built to vent the excessive heat thrown off by Nar Shaddaa's antiquated power plants, the stacks were one of the reasons why the city's residents had pushed their structures up and away from the moon's rocky surface.

Sweat poured off Kyle's body as he made his way down ancient stone stairs, passed through a shattered gate, and stepped over a strange-looking skeleton. The Rebel activated a glow rod and played the beam on the area in front of him.

Water was everywhere, dripping, gurgling, and gushing, as if part of a conspiracy to mask the sounds his enemies made. The agent swallowed and drew his blaster. Its weight was comforting.

A series of left-hand turns carried the Rebel away from the tower and out into a gap. An exhaust stack rose to Kyle's left, the remains of what appeared to be a temple appeared on the right, and a plaza opened in front of him.

The rain was warm and sticky. It soaked Kyle's hair and ran down his face. Moving cautiously, his eyes probing for movement, the agent edged his way forward. A landscape composed of puddles surrounded him. The rain churned them into miniature oceans with waves that dashed every which way.

Light gleamed off something, and Kyle used the back of his gun hand to wipe water from his brow. The glow rod wavered, touched something, and returned. Could it be? Yes, there it was! 88's arm was stump-down and fist-up! The disk glowed with reflected light.

Kyle splashed his way forward and was reaching for the disk when a Trandoshan exploded out of the water next to him. He was armed with a vibro-axe and knew how to use it. It seemed that what the Rebel had taken for a puddle was a good deal deeper — deep enough to hide a bounty hunter.

Kyle turned in the direction of his attacker, raised the blaster, and felt it struck from his hand.

The Trandoshan was proud of the manner in which he had disarmed his opponent on the upswing and planned to cleave the human's skull on the downstroke. One blow, one kill. Now, that's the way of the warrior!

Kyle, who had no desire to be split like a piece of firewood, dived to the side. He saw 88's arm and took it with him. Water broke the Rebel's fall, sprayed sideways, and rushed back in.

Furious at the manner in which the cowardly human sought to avoid what the bounty hunter saw as a righteous and well-deserved deathblow, the Trandoshan charged.

Kyle turned onto his back and instinctively raised his hands. The vibro-axe made a clanging sound as it hit 88's arm. The Trandoshan roared, raised his weapon, and went cross-eyed as Kyle kicked him between the legs.

The resulting splash brought help from the shadows. "Porg? Is that you? What's going on?"

Kyle swore, grabbed the bobbing glow rod, and turned it off. The agent felt the seconds tick away as he groped for the weapon's familiar outlines. Then he remembered the trick, the one he'd learned by accident and had used in the Rimmer's Rest. Would it work?

The agent forced himself to concentrate, to step outside his fear and *feel* the blaster in his hand. Suddenly it was there, butt-first, ready for use. He brought the weapon up out of the water and wondered if it would fire.

The Aqualish carried a light-mounted blast rifle and stomped out into the open as if he owned the place.

Kyle aimed just above the light, shot the bounty hunter in the chest, and watched the bolt bounce away. Body armor! A head shot, then . . .

The Trandoshan sat up. It was a poor decision. The Aqualish fired first — the human second. The Trandoshan took both bolts. Water boiled around the still-functioning vibro-axe.

The Aqualish was not only surprised but momentarily taken aback and paid the price. Kyle shot him in the head, paused to make sure of the kill, and took a moment to pry the disk out of 88's still-clenched fist.

Then, with the shouts of even more reinforcements ringing in his ears, Kyle decided to run. He knew the glow rod could betray his position. But he was forced to use it. It was either that or injure himself on unseen obstacles.

Kyle splashed through an ancient cemetery, wove between the rain-smoothed tombstones, and aimed for a dimly visible arch.

The noise was barely noticeable at first but grew in volume until it shook the ground under Kyle's feet. *Thump. Thump! THUMP!* It sounded like a heartbeat, as if the moon was alive and Kyle had discovered its pulse.

The source of the sound was a mystery at first but gradually revealed itself to be an upward spiraling ramp, outlined by widely spaced lights. It quickly became apparent that the conveyor belt emerged from deep within the planetoid's crust, followed the ramp upward, and delivered ore to the loading docks high above. Kyle had heard of the mines and knew they played an important part in Nar Shaddaa's history but had no idea that they were still operational.

While the Rebel didn't care about the mines or the ore they produced, the conveyor belt had definite possibilities.

He passed under the arch and climbed over piles of quietly rusting parts which, like the bones of some extinct monster, lay strewn where a machine had fallen fifty years before. Once free of their brooding presence, he headed straight for the point where the conveyor belt emerged from underground. A carefully sealed metal housing prevented access.

The agent located a ladder. It vibrated in sympathy with the machinery above. Kyle climbed quickly, arrived on a maintenance platform, and paused to check his back trail. Lights, it seemed like two or three, bobbed as they passed through the cemetery. Kyle swore and turned toward the belt.

The ore was reddish-orange in color and was moving at two or three kilometers an hour. Jumping onto the belt would be relatively easy. But then how to escape? He glanced over his shoulder. The lights were closer now — the first had cleared the cemetery.

Kyle secured his blaster and jumped.

The TIE fighters attacked the *Crow* within minutes after Jan cleared the tower. There were two of them, and, like the TIE bomber she had destroyed minutes before, they showed an amazing disregard for the safety of Nar Shaddaa's citizens. More of the same old arrogance — or desperation born of recent defeats? It was an interesting question but one best saved for later.

Jan put the *Crow* into a right-hand turn, placed the bulk of a large tower between the fighters and herself, and applied more power. Lights blurred meters away, and her back blast shattered a row of windows.

Sweat beaded Jan's forehead. What now? She couldn't fly in circles forever. There had to be a better way. Then she saw it, a distant spire still under construction, the top twenty floors waiting for walls.

Jan bit her lip as she dived into a well-lit canyon. The first TIE fighter cleared the building, tried a deflection shot, and missed. One end of a sky bridge sagged and fell. The free end slammed into a building, severed the last connection, and disappeared into the abyss.

Jan wondered how many had died and continued to pull the Imperials away. She zigzagged between buildings, opened a lead, and struggled to extend it. A few extra seconds. That was all she needed.

The spire soared toward space, a monument to someone's ego and the perfect place to hide. Jan killed the *Crow*'s navigational lights, put the ship into a sweeping curve, and approached the building from the other side.

It took every bit of her skill to dump the right amount of speed, guide the ship into a rectangular slot, and put her down.

The TIE fighters swept past the building, failed to spot her, and circled back. They were slower this time and more methodical but were looking for the wrong thing — a ship in flight. Jan waited, hoping to escape.

Then, one of the fighters spotted Jan — or, more likely, the heat generated by her engine — and came to investigate. Jan gritted her teeth, waited for the Imperial to fill the rectangle in front of her, and fired her cannon. The TIE fighter exploded. Flames blocked the Rebel's primary escape route.

Knowing the other ship would find her unless she moved, Jan lit the *Crow*'s repulsors and eased her sideways. There was a grating noise as the top surface of the hull scraped against the ceiling, followed by silence as the agent made the necessary adjustment and looked for a way to escape.

Energy flared as TIE fighter number two spotted the Rebel and fired. There wasn't much Jan could do . . . . unless . . .

As in all of Nar Shaddaa's high-rise buildings, there were turbolift shafts toward the center of the spire. *Large* turbolift shafts, capable of transporting tons of supplies to the levels above. This building was no exception.

Jan slid the *Crow* into one such shaft, heaved a sigh of relief, and blasted upward. The TIE fighter, still in position and still blasting away, seemed completely unaware as the Rebel vessel emerged from the top of the building and circled down. Cannons fired, and the TIE fighter hit the side of the building, exploded into flames, and fell like a comet. The wreckage lit the canyon below.

>─┤◆>──○──<◆├─<

Kyle stood knee-deep in ore, ducked to avoid a cross brace, and stared up through the gloom. He blinked as the rain hit his eyes. What was that structure, anyway? A cover — or something a good deal more ominous? Whatever it was made a lot of noise, as if the ore was being crushed, or forced through some kind of sorter.

Much as the agent had enjoyed the ride, he had no desire to get tangled up with the machinery. He waited for the next cross brace, jumped as hard as he could, and managed to get a grip. He did a chin-up, threw one leg across the girder, and pulled the rest of his body over the top.

A quick scan revealed a catwalk twenty meters away. All Kyle had to do was walk the length of the beam and climb aboard. He made the mistake of looking down. It was a long, long way. Lights bobbed as his pursuers climbed a maintenance ladder.

The Rebel swore, scooted along the beam, and transferred to the catwalk. It was a good decision, one that allowed him to travel faster. The catwalk led Kyle to a ladder which gave access to a maintenance platform and a nearby freight lift. Finally! Something he could rest on.

A wave of fatigue rolled over Kyle, and without the constant flow of adrenaline to keep him going, he collapsed in a corner. The lift stopped occasionally to allow a droid on or off, but there were no signs of pursuit. Did that mean what Kyle hoped? That he had worn them down? That the chase was over?

The platform slowed, the words "roof access" appeared on the indicator panel, and the lift came to a stop. Kyle struggled to his feet, waited for the doors to open, and peered outside. Nothing. He felt for the earpiece and the comm unit that it served. Both had disappeared, lost in the darkness below.

The doors started to close and buzzed when Kyle used his blaster to keep them apart. They sensed the resistance, opened, and allowed him to pass. The attack came without warning as a blaster bolt drilled a hole through Kyle's shoulder. He staggered and tried to respond but felt very, very tired. The blaster seemed so heavy that he could barely lift it. The bounty hunters were little more than a blur. He backpedaled, felt his shoulders hit the door, and waited for the shot that would end his life.

A voice sounded inside his head. "Go to the peace within. Nothing can touch you there. The Force will protect you."

Kyle had heard of the Force and instinctively knew that what he thought of as "the gun trick" relied on an energy source external to himself. That knowledge, plus extreme desperation, caused him to listen.

Kyle called on the Force, became one with it, and felt events start to slow. There was time now, plenty of time in which to assess the bounty hunters arrayed before him, raise his weapon, and open fire.

The Rebel felt removed somehow, like a witness to someone else's life. He watched as a Rodian toppled, a Gamorrean fell, and a human collapsed.

A feeling of smug invincibility settled over Kyle as his enemies fell like wheat before a scythe. No one could stand before him! No one was as smart, as powerful, as . . .

Suddenly, and without warning, the slow, almost dreamy battle snapped into fast forward. An energy beam sizzled past Kyle's head — and he understood his mistake. The Force was the source of his protection, not . . . A grenade exploded, the deck disappeared, and his head struck metal.

Jan had landed on the platform three hours before but had been forced to leave as other ships arrived. Astronomical fees, levied by the minute, left her no other choice.

That being the case, the Rebel had returned every half hour or so, landing when she could, scanning the area and calling over the radio when she couldn't.

It was a boring, frustrating duty — the kind she always wound up with — all because the only thing worse than working *with* Kyle was working without him.

The *Crow* was on final approach when the grenade went off. Jan saw the flash of light and guessed the rest. Kyle had arrived, and someone wanted to stop him. She goosed the drives and tried the comm. "*Crow* to Kyle — do you read me? Over."

Silence.

Jan felt her heart beat faster, brought the *Crow*'s weapons on-line, and pronounced a death sentence on anyone who tried to stop her.

The bounty hunters, those still standing after Kyle had thinned their ranks, heard the ship and turned. There were three of them, and they, plus the body slumped against the elevators, were all Jan needed to see.

Blasters winked as the Rebel kicked the ship to the left, fired the bow cannon, and swung the nose to the right. Coherent light stuttered out, punched holes through the bounty hunters' chests, and scorched the deck beyond. They staggered, spun, and fell, all without coming anywhere near Kyle's motionless body.

The *Crow* settled over the bounty hunters' bodies like a bird on carrion. The ramp fell, and Jan exited holding a blaster in each hand. A bounty hunter, the only one still alive, saw the expression on the agent's face and continued to play dead.

Jan, careful to keep an eye on her surroundings, made her way over to Kyle's still-unconscious body, stuck one of the blasters in its holster, and used her free hand to check his pulse. It was thready but steady. As with many blaster wounds, the hole had been cauterized as the energy bolt passed through it, and while caked with blood, Kyle's skull seemed intact.

Jan gave a sigh of relief, stuck the remaining blaster into her waistband, and grabbed Kyle under the armpits. Her partner's head flopped up and down as the agent dragged him to the ship and up the ramp. He was bigger than she, and Jan was forced to stop occasionally to regain her strength.

Finally, with the ramp retracted and Kyle secured in a bunk, she lifted off. The *Crow* swung out over the abyss, rose toward the blackness of space, and left Nar Shaddaa behind. Kyle needed help — and Jan would find it.

CHAPTER 4

The hospital ship *Mercy*, an antiquated Dreadnaught, two assault frigates, a squadron of Corellian gun ships, and assorted support vessels orbited a recently devastated world. Cities of colored glass, now reduced to rubble, merged with plains of heat-fused earth. This was just one of the many planets laid to waste during the last few years.

The *Mercy*, which had been "liberated" while still under construction, was enormous. More than two kilometers long and a quarter-kilometer across, she could accommodate up to five thousand patients plus the equipment, droids, and staff needed to operate and maintain her.

In spite of her considerable size however, the *Mercy* was badly overcrowded. More than six thousand Rebel casualties were crammed into her hull. They filled her wards and spilled out into the passageways, where they stood, sat, or lay on improvised beds. Even worse was the fact that patients who should have been immersed in one of the vessel's 4,250 bacta tanks were forced to wait.

It meant older, less effective medical procedures had to be brought into play. And that meant some of the wounded would suffer permanent disabilities since the longer bacta therapy was delayed the less effective it became.

Jan felt a lump in her throat as she threaded her way through packed corridors and caught glimpses of bodies cut in half, heads without faces, and beings so burned she couldn't determine whether they were human or members of another species.

The fact that she wasn't immortal, that she could have been one of them, made her stomach queasy. Jan knew she'd never forget the *Mercy* corridors, the sacrifices her fellow Rebels had made, or the true price of freedom.

It took fifteen minutes to reach bacta ward 114. Three replacement units had been pressed into service and placed out in the corridor. They contained what remained of a gun ship's twelve-person crew. The ship, the *GS-138*, had been ambushed while on a top-secret raid. Debris and some life pods were all that remained when help arrived.

The survivors — including a man, a woman, and a male Mon Calamari — were suspended in bacta and mercifully unconscious. Medals hung from the jury-rigged cables that connected their tanks to the ship's computerized monitoring systems. Notes, drawings, and snapshots were taped to the tanks. A tired-looking medic turned to greet her. He was balding and slightly overweight. "Yes?"

"I'm looking for a patient named Kyle Katarn."

Although there was no outward sign of its special status, ward 114 was reserved for members of the Alliance's Intelligence and Special Operations contingents. Though not especially nice to contemplate, the fact was that some casualties were considered more important than others, and Kyle — a proven if not completely trusted agent — was on the list of those slated to receive high-priority medical treatment. That being the case, certain security measures were in place.

The medic considered himself to be something of an expert where cloak and dagger types were concerned. The civilian flight suit, non-standard sidearm, and haunted eyes all pointed to one conclusion: a spy come to see a spy. They were jumpy at times, so it paid to be careful. The medic kept his voice neutral. "May I see your I.D.?"

Jan produced her card and watched it pass through the reader. The medic checked the readout and nodded toward a hatch. "Your friend is in tank twenty-three. We'll pull him later today. That's good, you know. He'll be up and around soon."

Jan thanked the medic, triggered the door, and stepped within. A maintenance droid was working on an empty tank, and aside from gentle tool noises, the ward was quiet. The air had a tangy smell which might have been pleasant if it weren't for the sights that went with it.

The tanks were numbered and contained things Jan didn't really want to see, things that floated like specimens in jars. Some appeared intact, but others bore obvious wounds. The agent was glad they were asleep.

Tank 23 looked like those around it except for the fact that no one had left any medals or notes on it. Kyle floated there, his body curled into the fetal position, his hair drifting like seaweed. He looked innocent, more boy than man.

The agent approached the unit and placed her hands on the tank's transparisteel surface. It was cool and damp, like recently showered skin or the hull of a starship. Something caught at the back of her throat as Jan remembered the three long days during which Kyle's condition had vacillated between good and bad. She had stabilized the shoulder wound, but the concussion led to vomiting and periods of unconsciousness, symptoms the ship's rather limited medical references flagged as serious.

But they made it to Rebel-held space, and while Kyle entered bacta tank 23, Jan collapsed on a cot. Twelve hours of sleep left her rested but concerned. She had no idea what Kyle had been up to in Nar Shaddaa or why he'd gone after the disk. This was not the sort of admission she wanted to make to their superiors. Especially when *she* was senior, and nominally in charge.

Each bacta tank had a small cupboard where personal items were kept. Jan knelt, tugged on the door, and pulled it open. Kyle's clothes were there along with his sidearm and boots. She rummaged through his pockets and came up with a wallet, a holo cube, and, yes, the mysterious disk.

Jan felt torn. It wasn't right to snoop through Kyle's belongings. But agents weren't supposed to *have* any privacy — not where their partners were concerned. In spite of the fact that Jan had complete trust in Kyle, it was hard to convince others that they should feel the same way, especially at times like this.

She triggered the holo projector, watched Morgan Katarn bid his son good-bye, and bit her lower lip. The wallet came next. She had glanced through the contents and was about to return it when she saw something unexpected. The agent came across a 3-D snapshot of herself! How and when had Kyle obtained it? There was no way to know. But the fact that it was there meant a lot.

Tears trickled down Jan's cheeks as she slipped the disk into her pocket, restored the rest of Kyle's belongings to the cabinet, and got to her feet. Her fingers left outlines on the transparisteel casing. The prints faded when she removed her hands. "I'm sorry, Kyle — I love you."

Then, walking fast, so as to complete the chore as quickly possible, Jan left the ward. The medic watched her go, wished someone cared enough to cry over *him*, and returned to his work. There were charts to update, and Lieutenant Commander Nidifer would check to make sure they were done.

>+<◆>+○+<◆>+<

Jan spent the better part of two hours trying to access the disk's contents but finally gave up. The contents were encrypted, and she couldn't break through. She needed help, expert help, the kind of help resident on the flagship.

Rather than request clearance for the *Crow* and fly the relatively short distance to the *New Hope* Jan decided to take advantage of a regularly scheduled shuttle. The trip to the refurbished Dreadnaught took less than fifteen minutes. Once aboard, the agent went in search of an old acquaintance, a friend of her father's, presently in charge of the flagship's Electronic Counter Measures section. His name was Chief Warrant Officer Xiong Wong, "Chiefy" to his friends and "that miserable old geezer" to those who abused his equipment and were caught at it.

She found Chiefy the same way she always did, by asking his subordinates where the trouble was and descending into the bowels of the ship. After that, it was a simple matter to follow a trail of temporarily abandoned tools through a crawl space and into a floodlit equipment bay. The Warrant Officer, along with two of his techs, was hard at work. Cables squirmed into the space from five or six directions and converged on an open junction box.

Chiefy took one look at her, gave a whoop of joy, and offered to buy her lunch — a purely symbolic invitation, since anyone could enter the chow hall free of charge.

Jan accepted, ignored the stares, and followed Wong out. There was very little chance that he could access the disk. But he'd know people who could.

Kyle awoke between clean, crisp sheets. He remembered the bacta tank — but it was nowhere to be seen. Sleep pulled him down. He dreamt of his father's home, of Jan staring at him through a window, of a man he'd never seen before. The man had dark skin and wore a plain white robe. There was something about his voice, about the way that he spoke, that captured Kyle's attention.

"A crossroads lies before you. . . . The same man who murdered your father contemplates an even greater evil. His name is Jerec, and he seeks a place called the Valley of the Jedi, a place where thousands of Jedi spirits are trapped, a place of almost unbelievable power, a place he must never reach. Because if he does — the results could be catastrophic. Imagine someone who could destroy a star with a whisper, eradicate a solar system with a snap of his fingers, or 'think' a planet from its orbit.

"Your father gave his life to protect this place . . . and the power it contains. His destiny was linked with it . . . and your destiny is linked with his.

"Your apprenticeship has been underway for some time now. The disk will help you absorb the ways of the Jedi. Learn them well, and learn them quickly, for time is short."

Rahn faded from sight, strange-looking rock formations appeared, and Kyle struggled to see. The image steadied for a moment, slipped from focus, and faded away. The name Jerec meant something, but he couldn't remember what. Kyle was thinking about that, or trying to, when sleep pulled him down, again.

>–∙◄►∙–○–∙◄►∙–◄

Chief Warrant Officer Xiong Wong used a hydrospanner to bang on the hatch. "Hey, Wires, I know you're in there, so open up."

Silence.

Wong looked at Jan and winked. "Don't worry. I have a surefire way to get his attention." The spanner banged again.

"Okay, Wires. Have it your way. Lieutenant Commander Olifer seems like a reasonable man. . . . The fact that you have appropriated thirty-two percent of the tracking computer's excess capacity for your own personal gain won't bother him in the least."

The hatch jerked open, and a small man with a long, thin nose peered out. He had small, beady eyes. They ran the length of Jan's body and flicked to Wong. "What's the problem, Chiefy? I'm busy."

"Busy running a virtual gambling casino," Wong said equably. "Not that I care — as long as your computer's combat ready."

"So? You came to tell me that?"

"No," Chiefy replied calmly, "I came to get your help on this." Wong held the disk between thumb and forefinger. Light winked off its surface. "It's read-protected, and my friend wants in."

Wires looked from the disk to the Warrant Officer's face. "I crack it, and you leave me alone?"

"Affirmative."

"And Olifer?"

"Remains blissfully ignorant until you get greedy and give yourself away."

"Done. Let's get on with it."

Jan spent the next two hours in the overcrowded storeroom which Wires had converted to his own nefarious purposes. There was little to nothing the agent could do to help, but she felt obliged to stay. Partly because Chiefy had, and partly because Wires was clearly untrustworthy.

The computer expert knew what he was doing, but it was slow going, nonetheless. First, he applied some off-the-shelf encryption software. It didn't work. More than a little angry now, and a good deal more engaged, Wires tried again. The next program he ran made use of software he had written himself. Even that didn't work the first time through, although Jan did catch a glimpse of a middle-aged man who looked a lot like Morgan Katarn.

Finally, with a whoop of triumph, Wires made a partial breakthrough. It was like staring through a snowstorm, and the static made some of the words hard to hear, but there was no mistaking what was said.

Jan swore both men to secrecy, took the original *and* the partially decoded copy, and gave Chiefy a hug. Wires looked as though he would have enjoyed a hug, too, but was forced to settle for a handshake. The walk from the storeroom to the Dreadnaught's bridge was one of the longest Jan had ever made.

Like the Dreadnaught herself, the cabin dated back to pre-Imperial days and was extremely spacious — fitting quarters for an admiral whose duties were mainly ceremonial.

The ship had been something of a fixture over Churba, where it had functioned as an orbital war museum until it was "liberated" by the Rebels and refitted. There were no resources to squander on decor, however, which explained why the same tapestries that had graced the bulkheads prior to the Rebellion still hung there, adding to the somewhat musty smell. Mon Mothma had grown used to the odor, but Leia Organa, formerly *Princess* Organa, hadn't. She sneezed, and her brother, Luke Skywalker, said, "Bless you."

Mon Mothma, who was deeply engaged in a logistical problem, took scant notice. Sneezes and what people said about them were less important than medical supplies and the systems used to distribute them. Mon Mothma wore her hair short so as to minimize maintenance and preferred loose-fitting robes — worn with a single clasp or pin — to the tunics and trousers that Leia favored. Perhaps it was a habit picked up during her years as a senator or — and this seemed more likely — it was a matter of comfort. Whatever the reason, the administrator's robes swished this way and that as she strode back and forth.

"And so," she continued, "the efficient distribution of medical supplies not only will save lives, it will signal the government's priorities *and* our ability to deliver on them."

Luke, who knew he should care about such matters, struggled to pay attention. The administrative and political matters that Mon Mothma and his sister found so fascinating often left him cold or, more accurately, bored. That being the case, he looked hopeful when one of Mon Mothma's aides slipped into the compartment and whispered something into the administrator's ear. Any sort of distraction would be welcome. The administrator listened, nodded, and said something in return.

The aide left, and Mon Mothma turned to her guests. "Excuse the interruption, but it seems as though something rather urgent has come up."

Leia and Luke rose as if to leave, and Mon Mothma gestured for them to stay. "No. I would appreciate your opinions on this."

The hatch opened, and a woman entered. Leia noticed she was pretty, though not self-consciously so, and dressed in a civilian flight suit. The fact that she had passed through a security check and still wore a sidearm testified to her clearance. Mon Mothma gave the newcomer a hug and turned to her guests. "Jan, this is Leia Organa and her brother Luke Skywalker. . . . Leia, Luke, this is Jan Ors. It was Jan who, along with an agent named Kyle Katarn, stole the Death Star plans from the lab on Danuta."

Jan felt blood rush to her cheeks. Leia Organa? As in *Princess* Leia Organa? And *Luke Skywalker*? The Jedi Knight? Both were famous. She wasn't sure what kind of reception she would get.

But there was no mistaking their enthusiasm, the warmth of Leia's handshake, or the grin on Skywalker's face as they circled the table to greet her. "This is a *real* pleasure. . . . What you did took guts. And it saved a lot of lives. Thank you."

Jan blushed all over again, stammered something about how Kyle had carried out the most difficult part of the mission, and was glad when Mon Mothma brought the conversation back to the present. "You have something to report? Something about a valley?"

Jan nodded. "It's called the Valley of the Jedi."

Luke sat up straight. "What did you say? The Valley of what?"

Alarmed and somewhat taken aback, Jan repeated the name. "The Valley of the Jedi . . . Why? Have you heard of it?"

Luke looked thoughtful. "Yes, I've heard of it. First from Yoda. And then from others. None of them had actually seen it, though . . . and that makes me wonder."

Jan shrugged and held the disk up for them to see. "Well, Kyle's father thought it was real and left a message to that effect."

Leia frowned. "*Thought* it was real? What happened to him?"

Jan remembered the holo she and Kyle had seen on board the *Star of Empire* and winced. "The Imperials murdered Morgan Katarn and placed his head on a spike."

Luke raised an eyebrow. "He was *beheaded*? That's how they killed him?"

"I guess so. Does it make a difference?"

The Jedi's bionic hand strayed to the lightsaber at his side. "Maybe, and maybe not," he replied vaguely. "But it's my observation that beheadings are as rare as the weapons used to carry them out."

Jan was just starting to consider the implications of that when Mon Mothma gestured toward the disk. "Let's see what Katarn has to say."

Jan apologized for the quality and dropped the disk into a player. What looked like a snowstorm swirled, static crackled, and an image appeared. The man had gray, almost white hair, and a full growth of beard. His eyes were kindly but tired. A workshop or similar area appeared in the background.

"This message is intended for my son Kyle Katarn —" *crackle . . . pop . . . crackle . . .* "— Kyle, I have left two very important items for you. The first is a map to the Valley of the Jedi, which is embedded in the stone ceiling above this room. The other is a lightsaber that once belonged to a Jedi named Rahn. Use it well. Use it for good."

Mon Mothma knew Rahn and wondered where he was. Luke had heard of the Jedi from Yoda.

Leia broke the silence. "No offense to you or the Katarn family, but so what? Why should the Alliance get involved? Resources are scarce. They must be allocated with care." Mon Mothma nodded in agreement.

Jan felt defensive and tried to conceal it. "The Imperials care, so we should care. They tried to keep the disk, lost it to Kyle, and fought to get it back. That's the best answer I can give."

Luke intervened before Leia could reply. "Listen to the legend, and you will understand."

Mon Mothma started to say something and thought better of it. Luke continued. "Hundreds and hundreds of years ago a Jedi named Kaan turned away from the light and formed the Brotherhood of Darkness. The Brotherhood used the dark side of the Force to build an empire and were well on their way toward expanding it when an army was raised to oppose them.

"The army of opposition consisted of beings from many species and planets, representing all walks of life. But they had one thing in common. They were Jedi.

"The two sides came together on a remote and little-known world. Salvos of pure energy were exchanged, storms raged across the land, and lightning flashed from the skies. Entire cities were destroyed, a species was pushed to the edge of extermination, and spirits separated from their bodies.

"Finally, after days of mortal combat, the Brotherhood was defeated. Knowing that he had lost but unwilling to accept defeat, Kaan lured his opponents into a valley. And it was there that the Brotherhood of Darkness committed suicide, taking good Jedi with them. Not to the freedom of death but into a state of suspended animation where they remain trapped.

"Their spirits should be released and allowed to merge with the Force, but there are those who would tap the energy they represent and use it for evil. Assuming the stories are true, assuming such a place exists, it would be well worth fighting for."

There was momentary silence as the rest of the group took the story in. Jan was the first to speak. "Kyle will be up and around soon. We'll find the map."

Mon Mothma shook her head. "I don't think that's a very good idea, Jan. Kyle needs time to heal."

Leia saw the way Jan's eyes narrowed, the manner in which her mouth formed a hard, straight line, and knew the agent disagreed. What she didn't know was the extent to which Jan had matured over the last year or so, giving her the courage to challenge Mon Mothma's authority.

"With all due respect, agents are wounded all the time and thrown into action the moment they can walk. If this is about Kyle and the fact that he was an Imperial officer, then say so."

The fact that the agent in question had been a member of the Imperial military forces was news to Leia and Luke. They exchanged glances but remained silent. Mon Mothma felt no such compunction. "All right, it may not be fair, but I don't trust him. He's a graduate of the Imperial Military Academy. How can we be sure of his loyalty?"

Leia looked from one woman to the other and said what she felt. "Han was a smuggler, and some say worse. *He* graduated from the Academy, yet you trust him. People can and do change."

Jan shot Leia a grateful look. It confirmed what Leia had suspected all along. Jan Ors was in love with Kyle Katarn — for better or worse.

If Mon Mothma was annoyed, she gave no sign of it. "So, Luke, you've heard both sides of the issue. What do you think?"

The Jedi stared at the floor, lost in thought. His words came slowly, as if from a distance. "I think the second part of the message bears on the first. What did Katarn say? Something about a lightsaber that belonged to Rahn? The gift implies talent — talent and something more — connections that I sense but can't put into words. I believe we can trust Kyle. The real question is whether he can trust himself. A self-taught Jedi? A great deal could go wrong. Still, the path is his, and he must walk it."

Mon Mothma looked thoughtful for a moment and turned to Jan. "Say nothing of this meeting. Allow Kyle to do as he will. If he's even half the man you say he is, all will be well. If he turns on us — kill him. Agreed?"

Kyle? Jedi? Was such a thing possible? And what about Mon Mothma's orders? Jan remembered Danuta — and the moment when she had pointed her blaster at Kyle's head. She hadn't been able to do it then. Could she do it now? Probably not. But she nodded anyway. "Agreed."

Leia saw the lie and allowed herself the tiniest of smiles. Life had never been, and never would be, simple.

Kyle hovered somewhere between sleep and wakefulness. He heard the medic enter the room, watched her through carefully slitted eyes, and maintained his silence. The shoulder wound felt better, *much* better, but he was in no mood to talk.

The medic glanced in his direction as if to make sure that the agent was all right and turned her attention to the officer in the next bed. Tubes snaked in and out of his body, and the respirator made a gentle wheezing sound as it pushed oxygen into his lungs. The medic checked to make sure everything was operating properly, tapped some readings into a datapad, and left the compartment.

Kyle allowed himself to drift and was just about to take still another nap when someone entered. The medic? Back already? He peered through half-closed eyes.

Jan came in, looked around, and approached the foot of his bed. She looked just plain wonderful — pretty in spite of the coveralls she wore, yet pensive, as if she was worried about something.

Kyle was about to greet Jan, to tell her he felt better, when she turned away. Two lockers, one for each patient, were bolted to the bulkhead. Jan opened Kyle's, removed his trousers, and slipped her hand into a pocket. Then, after placing a kiss on his forehead, she left.

Kyle waited to make sure she wouldn't return, swung his feet over the side of the bed, and got to his feet. The deck was cold and hard. He opened the locker, grabbed his pants, and checked the pockets. Everything, including the all-important disk, was just as he'd left it. Or was it? What was Jan doing anyway? And if she had removed something — only to replace it — what had it been? His wallet? The disk? The holo cube? And why?

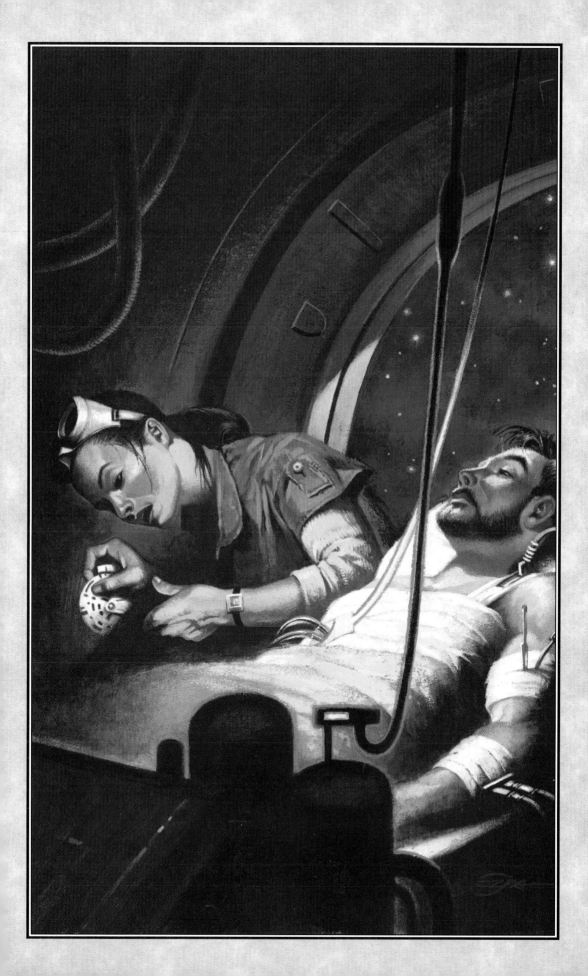

The agent frowned, shucked his gown, and started to dress. The disk, the dream, and Jan. The pieces were in front of him. But how did they fit? The answer was out there — and he would find it.

CHAPTER 5

Sullust hung huge in the sky as Boc stood watching the troops guide the heavily loaded grav pallet up the ramp and into the shuttle's hold. The tiles were numbered and ready for reassembly. He shifted his weight and winced in pain.

The ache originated from the point where his tendon had been severed and reconnected. Boc favored his opposite foot as he turned to Yun. "That was the last load."

The younger Jedi nodded. "What now?"

"Here comes Sariss. . . . Ask her."

Yun turned toward his mentor. "And to what fabulous destination are we bound?"

"To Baron's Hed, so 8t88 can examine the map and try to make sense of it."

"Ah," Yun replied lightly, "and a fine piece of machinery he is. . . . Come, Boc. The bright lights beckon."

There was no answer.

Yun and Sariss turned to see where the other Jedi had gone. He stood with his back to them. His eyes scanned the countryside. Yun spoke again. "Boc? Come on — it's time to go."

"Someone is watching. I can feel it."

"So?" Sariss responded impatiently. "What did you expect? This is more activity than the locals have seen for a long time. We're hard to miss."

"The Force is strong in this one," Boc continued, "and he seeks to destroy us."

"Him and a few million more," Yun said dismissively. "Come. Lunch awaits."

"Into the shuttle, Boc," Sariss ordered sternly. "Jerec wants the map, and he wants it soon." Boc took one last look, turned, and shuffled toward the ramp. The remaining Jedi exchanged glances, shook their heads in wonderment, and followed.

⋟━┼━◆━┼━○━┼━◆━┼━⋞

Kyle couldn't hear what the Imperials were saying. And he didn't really care. From his vantage point up on the hill he could see the fields, the tap tree that stood in front of the house, and the Imperial shuttle that squatted beyond. Heat shimmered above the ship's hull and distorted the vehicle parked beyond. It contained a half-dozen transports, some gravsleds, and a mobile command post.

Timing was everything, or so the saying went, and his had been poor. The heavily loaded grav pallets meant that the Imperials had removed something. But what? Whatever it was would have to be a good deal more valuable than his father's tools and equipment to justify the expenditure of so many resources.

Kyle felt a momentary sense of pride. The Empire had murdered Morgan Katarn — but his impact lingered on.

It appeared as though the Imperials were preparing to leave. Some of them, anyway. The agent raised his electrobinoculars and took one last look. Two men and a woman stood in front of the shuttle. They were Jedi, judging from the lightsabers they wore. But none was Jerec. Where was he anyway, the mysterious figure who had attended Kyle's graduation, murdered his father, and sent 8t88 to find him? Close, very close, but out of reach.

Kyle touched a button and zoomed to maximum magnification. He examined each Jedi in turn. The woman wore bright red lipstick, the youngster displayed an "I'm better than you are" sneer, and the last was a Twi'lek, a rarity among Imperial forces. The alien turned toward Kyle. The agent felt his heart start to pound as he made contact with the space-black eyes.

Kyle lowered the electrobinoculars, certain that he'd been discovered. But he realized that he hadn't. Not in the normal sense, anyway. . . .

The others spoke to the strange-looking Jedi, and he turned away. Kyle felt light-headed and fought to control his breathing. The encounter had been frightening and exhilarating at the same time. Here was partial validation of his dream. Maybe, just maybe, he could become a Jedi — not the kind that murdered people but the kind that fought to protect them.

The Jedi, along with a contingent of stormtroopers, had boarded the shuttle by now, and the ship was lifting. Repulsors flared, the nose rotated toward the east, and thrusters fired.

Kyle went facedown as the shuttle passed directly over his position. Bushes swayed and dust filled the air. The Rebel looked back over his shoulder, spit grass, and was thankful when the spacecraft disappeared.

He stood, gave thanks that Jan hadn't been around to witness his rather undignified dive, and brushed grass off his clothes.

A quick check confirmed that although the Jedi had left, stormtroopers and mercenaries still patrolled the area around the house while an AT-ST minced through an unplanted field.

Tough odds, but not impossible ones, especially for someone who had spent his childhood there and knew every square centimeter.

Kyle checked his blaster, shoved it back into its holster, and moved along the side of the hill. Imperial troops had a strong tendency to do everything by the book, and having studied their books, he knew what to expect.

Sentries would be posted all around the structure to be defended. Not many, just enough to slow an incursion and call for reinforcements. Once that occurred, a heavily armed response force would rush to the area and provide whatever muscle was necessary.

That being the case, Kyle hoped to slip between the sentries and avoid the massive response. He stayed off the well-established footpaths and took the sort of routes that only a child would be aware of, routes that were much more likely to be free of sentries, sensors, and trip wires. One such path, which was little more than a game trail now, required Kyle to get down on his stomach and elbow his way forward. Bushes closed over his head and brushed his sides.

The going was a good deal more difficult than he remembered. Of course, now he had an adult body, and the undergrowth had closed in on itself during his absence.

The smells were the same, though, especially the yeasty odor of wild poro poppies and the sweet, almost nauseating scent of nantha blossoms.

Insects scurried to get out of his way.

A harmless eye-eye snake hissed, aimed its head-eye in the direction of travel, and used the tail-eye to monitor pursuit.

A hole ball, its fur eternally matted with the debris that provided its camouflage, took one look at the enormous invader, gave a squeak of alarm, and rolled into one of its multitudinous holes.

Kyle smiled. All the creatures around him were old friends, or descendants of old friends, first encountered during his boyhood.

The undergrowth thinned, and the farmhouse appeared through the foliage. The Rebel squirmed his way forward, spotted a patch of telltale white armor, and ceased all movement.

The stormtrooper paused, scanned the surrounding area, and resumed his patrol. Kyle waited for the sentry to leave, pushed his way forward, and stuck his head out. The way was clear, except for a blaster-burned, agro droid.

Kyle dashed across the intervening space, tried the back door, and felt it open under his hand. The lock, such as it was, had been blasted away.

The kitchen was a disaster. Cupboard doors gaped open, graffiti covered the walls, and debris crunched under his boots. The agent paused, listened, and moved on.

It appeared as if the house had been ransacked on repeated occasions. The Imperials had been first, followed by thieves who'd seen Morgan Katarn's head on display at the spaceport, then people with nothing better to do.

Someone had camped in the living room. A collection of dirty pots and pans was stacked next to the fireplace, and trash filled the northeast corner of the room. More than a little nervous, Kyle made his way to the front room and peered out the window. A Commando appeared, and the Rebel pulled back.

Getting in was one thing — getting out would be another. Still, no one had shown any inclination to enter the house, for which he was thankful. Perhaps most of them had been there already or had orders to stay out. Whatever the reason, it was fine with Kyle.

A trail of masonry drew a line between the much-abused front door and Morgan Katarn's workshop. Kyle followed it until a picture caught his eye. It hung askew, as if ready to fall. Not too surprising, given what the place had been through.

Kyle walked over, removed the 3-D print from the wall, and gazed into his mother's face. He had a single memory of her — of being held in her arms, of crying over something, something that didn't seem so bad with her arms wrapped around him.

Tenderly, reverently, Kyle removed the picture from its frame and rolled it into a cylinder. A scrap of wire served to secure the roll, which went into his right cargo pocket. It might take a beating during the hours ahead, but anything was preferable to leaving the print where it was.

The agent entered the workshop. His father and he had spent

countless hours there, taking things apart, putting them back together, or just plain fooling around. The shop had been the center of the house and, in some ways, of their relationship.

A single glance was enough to determine that it, too, had suffered at the hands of the invaders. It appeared as though at least one minor explosion had taken place. The vast majority of his father's tools were missing, and a thick layer of debris obscured the floor. Of course, that was to be expected. But where had the ceiling gone? And why?

Kyle remembered the heavily laden grav pallets and wondered if the two were connected somehow. But wait — what was that? A pattern on the remaining ceiling tiles?

Kyle removed a glow rod from his belt, climbed up onto an empty crate, and examined the area in question. He noticed that the tiles, none of which had been there on the day he left for the Academy, matched those on the kitchen counters. That meant they had originated in the same quarry — a place located twenty kilometers to the north. Etchings had been carved into the squares, some of which were clearly decorative, while others resembled a map — a map from which the central and most important section was missing.

What had Rahn said? Something about the Valley of the Jedi? Was that what the Imperials had come for? A map that would guide them to the Valley? There was no direct evidence to support his theory, but Kyle *felt* it was true and had learned to trust such impressions.

The agent climbed down, directed the light into one of the darker corners of the room, and saw something familiar. It was covered with loose plaster but was recognizable, nonetheless. "Wee Gee? Is that you?"

There was no answer as Kyle made his way across the room, scooped chunks of plaster out of the way, and embraced a familiar figure. Though capable of a wide variety of configurations, the droid currently resembled an inverted *U* with a sensor pod mounted on top. Wee Gee boasted two graspers, one designed for strength and one intended for more delicate tasks. Kyle dragged the droid out into the middle of the room and checked its readouts.

"Hey, Weeg — what did they do to you? Whatever it was put some dents in your processor housing. No major damage, though. Let's check you out."

Morgan Katarn had built the droid himself, but Kyle had performed routine maintenance on the robot since the age of twelve and knew its workings inside out. Beyond the dirt, grime, and dents, the machine was intact.

The half slots seemed unrelated to each other until Kyle rotated

both of them into alignment and pushed the disk through the opening. Parts whirred, clicked, and hummed. A holo appeared, and with it, his father's image. It was crystal clear.

"This message is intended for my son, Kyle Katarn. Kyle, I have left two very important items for you. The first is a map to the Valley of the Jedi — and is embedded in the stone ceiling above this room. . . . "

Kyle watched his father gesture toward the once-smooth ceiling and knew his theory had been correct. Something whirred; the agent turned and pulled his blaster. Wee Gee remained motionless. A hatch opened in his side, and a cylinder popped out. The agent caught the object and the narration continued. "The other is a lightsaber that belonged to a Jedi named Rahn. Use it well. Use it for good."

The holo snapped out of existence. A feeling of warmth suffused Kyle's body. Not only would the new image replace the one of his father's head on a spike, it meant that his father had been aware of his talent and wanted him to develop it.

Kyle thumbed a switch, and the lightsaber popped to life. The air crackled, and the smell of ozone permeated the room. He made some experimental passes, gloried in the power that the weapon conveyed, and heard his father's words echo through his mind. "Use it well. . . . Use it for good."

The thought had a sobering effect, as did the knowledge that the Imperials had taken possession of information that his father had gone to great lengths to protect. He thumbed the power switch, felt the handle cool, and stuck the lightsaber through his belt.

There was a series of beeps and whistles. The agent turned to find Wee Gee floating two meters off the floor. The droid held a chunk of rock in his power grasper and seemed prepared to throw it. "Hey, Weeg. It's me, Kyle."

The droid seemed doubtful and moved in for a closer look. The beeps and whistles had a plaintive sound.

Kyle shook his head. "I *look* older because I *am* older. Not too old to remember how you fished me out of the river, though, and didn't tell Dad."

The droid responded with a series of quick, joyful sounds. Kyle patted the droid's sensor housing. "You've been out of circulation for a while Weeg, and things have changed. I'd like nothing better than to see Dad again, but the Imperials murdered him. I'm fighting for the Rebs now."

It took the better part of five minutes to bring the droid up to date. Once that had been accomplished and Wee Gee had absorbed all the changes, it was Kyle's turn to ask the questions.

"So, Weeg, what's the deal with the ceiling? What made it so valuable that the Imperials would take the time and trouble to tear it out?"

The droid directed its vid pickup toward the area in question and issued a long sequence of beeps and whistles. The Rebel made the necessary translation. It seemed that his father had taken a long trip and had seemed preoccupied on his return. It was as if he knew of something important but wasn't sure what to do about it. The droid continued.

"Later, after Master Rahn came to stay, your father worked on the ceiling. It took more than a month, and I helped. I liked the etchings. But your father must not have because he ordered me to cover them with plaster."

Kyle felt his heart beat faster. "Rahn? A man named Rahn came to stay?"

"Why, yes," the droid beeped. "A wonderful gentleman. Your father thought very highly of him."

Kyle's mouth was dry. "Describe Master Rahn."

Wee Gee projected a holo into the air. A lump formed in Kyle's throat as he watched the man he knew as Rahn hand a book and a lightsaber to Morgan Katarn. Their friendship was obvious.

Kyle swallowed hard. In spite of all he'd learned, the main prize continued to elude him. Given the fact that the shuttle had disappeared in the direction of Baron's Hed, that seemed like the place to start. But how to get there? Especially with Wee Gee in tow. Yes, he could leave the droid behind, but he knew what would happen. Wee Gee was like a member of the family, the only member left outside of himself, and couldn't survive on his own. No, there had to be a way. . . .

The answer popped into his mind as if it had been waiting there all along. Kyle snapped his fingers and motioned to the droid. "Come on, Weeg. Let's get out of here."

The towering tap tree that stood out front was more than ornamental. Its roots went down hundreds of meters, where they "tapped" an underground aquifer and brought water to the surface. *More* water than the tree and its various symbiotes could use. That being the case, Morgan Katarn and his neighbors had used the trees as biological pumps, diverting the excess water to their crops and supplementing the sometimes inadequate rainfall.

However, bringing the water to the surface was one thing and distributing it to the crops was another. Like his neighbors, Morgan Katarn employed a force of droids to establish and maintain an extensive network of underground tunnels, pipes, and tubes, which took the wet stuff wherever it was needed. The system could be accessed from a number of locations, one of which was located not ten meters from the back door.

The agent made his way through the kitchen, pushed against the door in question, and peered through the crack. A stormtrooper stood five meters away. A mercenary sauntered up to greet him. The Gamorrean had green skin, a pig-style snout, and some nasty-looking tusks. He wore a bloodsucking morrt on each bicep — an indication that he had put a few credits aside and was coming up in the world. He made some grunting noises, and the human responded. "Hey, Brollo. It's been a while. You ready to lose this week's pay?"

The Gamorrean's response was lost as Kyle backed into the room. Which was more important, stealth — or time? The Rebel considered the Jedi, how easy it would be for them to leave the planet, and made the decision accordingly.

"Weeg, see the door? When I say 'go,' pile through it and turn to the left. Don't go right, 'cause you'll be in the line of fire. Got it?"

Servos whined as the droid positioned himself opposite the back door and beeped his readiness.

Kyle nodded, pulled his blaster, and took one last peek. The trooper had removed a datapad from his pocket and pointed at the screen. "So, who do you want? Your cousin Blotho — or Master Sergeant Kine? The smart money's on Kine."

The agent pulled back. "Okay, Weeg . . . ready . . .set . . .go!"

Kyle had expected the droid to pull the door open and was just as surprised as the Imperials were when Wee Gee crashed *through* the wood, leaving nothing but splinters hanging from the hinges. There was no time to discuss the matter, however — and the strategy worked.

The Imperials were still recovering from the shock, still reaching for their weapons when Kyle shot them. The Gamorrean died first, his face registering surprise, and the trooper fell second. It took three shots to penetrate his armor, but the outcome was the same.

Kyle turned, pulled a quick three-sixty to ensure that the incident had gone undetected, and headed for the access door, which lay flush to the ground, where layers of dirt and debris served to camouflage it. Kyle found the handle and tugged. Nothing. It was jammed tight.

Wee Gee beeped, whistled, and moved into position. The droid's power grasper slipped through the handle, and a servo whined. Metal groaned as the door opened upward, and a set of stairs was revealed. "Down the hatch," Kyle ordered, "and switch on your lights."

The droid beeped obediently and lowered itself into the underground passageway. Kyle pulled the door into a vertical position and ducked as it fell the last couple of meters. He'd be very lucky — or the Imperials extremely stupid — if the hatch went undiscovered.

It was dark in the tunnel, or would have been if it weren't for Wee Gee and his floodlights. Together they lit up fifteen to twenty meters of tunnel.

The earthen walls still bore the tool marks left by the droids who had dug and subsequently maintained the tunnels. They weeped here and there as water from a recent rainstorm percolated downward.

Side tunnels, some of which were too small for the adult Kyle to negotiate, branched left and right. Black pipes or, in some cases, tubing followed them off into the darkness. The air was moist and smelled like dirt. This particular shaft, a passageway labeled "main central" led toward the northwest and the area where the vehicle park had been established. The perfect place to borrow some transportation . . .

The attack came without warning. The passageway was empty one moment and full the next. The war droid was a lumbering thing, long outdated but threatening, nonetheless. There was no way to know if it had been *sent* into the tunnels or had simply lost its way. Whatever the reason, the machine had sensed their approach, lain in wait, and lurched out of a side passage.

The machine could and probably would have killed Kyle within the first few seconds of combat, but Wee Gee was a more difficult opponent. Though extremely mild mannered and not equipped for combat, the droid had been programmed by Morgan Katarn to protect Kyle at all costs. That, plus the fact that Wee Gee had been built for heavy-duty farm work, evened the odds.

Metal rang on metal as the machines came together. The war droid boasted a variety of weapons but discovered it was too late to use them.

Kyle tried to see past Wee Gee, waved his blaster, and shouted advice — none of which was very useful.

The matter was really quite simple from Wee Gee's perspective. Lacking the programming and initiative to do anything else, his opponent was using tactics that might have been effective against a human but were wasted on him.

While the war droid went for Wee Gee's nonexistent vital organs, Wee Gee used his power grasper to grab the other machine's throat and rip its head off. A column of sparks shot upward, a servo screeched, and the battle was over.

Wee Gee passed over the decapitated hulk, beeped a warning, and continued on his way.

Kyle shook his head in amazement, stepped on the war droid's chest, and followed along behind.

Cautious now, with blaster drawn and mud sucking at his boots, Kyle waited for another attack. But, with the exception of a small cave-in, there were no more obstacles to bar the way. Wee Gee plowed through the blockage without difficulty and stopped when the tunnel came to an abrupt end. The whistles, beeps, and buzz ended with a nearly audible question mark.

"Now I reconnoiter," Kyle answered, indicating a ladder and the hatch above. "If memory serves, this should bring us out in the center of their vehicle park."

The droid's vidcam swiveled back and forth as various aspects of his programming came into conflict and made him nervous. The noises he produced were hard and demanding.

"Thank you," Kyle replied sincerely, "but my father is gone now, and I would appreciate it if you would accept my judgments in place of his."

There was a brief moment of silence while Wee Gee considered Kyle's request. The reply was both brief and contrite.

"Good," Kyle said firmly. "I'll take a look — you wait here."

The droid watched as the Rebel agent climbed the rusty ladder, shoved on the hatch, and shoved again. Kyle grimaced as metal screeched and the cover popped free. He waited to see if the noise drew any attention and was relieved when it didn't.

The agent pushed upward on the lid, stopped when it hit something solid, and squirmed through the gap. The "something" was a transport. He'd been lucky, *very* lucky, since there were plenty of Imperials, and the vehicle hid him from view.

A pair of shiny black boots crunched by, a comm unit crackled, and someone coughed. Then, with a suddenness that made the agent's heart skip a beat, a shout was heard. Had he been spotted? The Rebel rolled this way and that, looking for someone to shoot. . . . But the boots, and the bodies above them, were running away. Running toward the house. Why?

Then it came to him. Someone had discovered the bodies and alerted the rest. How long before they found the hatch — and followed the tunnel to the point where Wee Gee waited? Not very long.

Kyle knew that seconds were precious as he elbowed his way out from under the vehicle, took a quick look around, and saw nothing but backs as stormtroopers, mercenaries, and commandos headed for the house.

The T-4 was a large vehicle with an open cab. Normally used to move equipment and troops, it boasted a five-ton payload, light side armor, and a double-barreled, all-purpose, energy cannon mounted behind the cab.

Kyle jumped onto the running board, climbed into the driver's seat, and scanned the dashboard. Like his classmates, he had qualified in T-4s during his second year at the Academy. The transport boasted no fewer than four repulsor-lift engines and, like most military vehicles, was secured with a key pad. A key pad which many company commanders chose to ignore since it meant that each and every potential driver had to memorize the necessary code. The factory setting consisted of four zeros. Many settings were just left that way.

Kyle mentally crossed his fingers, hit the zero button four times, and received a green light. The Rebel grinned as he flipped all four of the engine-select switches into the "on" position, hit the starter button, and heard the power plants whine into life. Each had its own special pitch that was soon lost in the sound made by the others.

Once the T-4 was up off its skids, it was a simple matter to slide out of the way and watch Wee Gee float up and out of his hiding place. The moment the droid was aboard and secured to his seat, Kyle took off.

A mercenary yelled something incoherent, the Imperials turned to look, and the chase was on. . . . Blaster bolts sizzled past the agent's head, and one of them punched a hole through the windshield. Wee Gee issued a series of urgent whistles and beeps.

"Excellent advice," Kyle replied grimly. "Hold on to your circuits . . . because here we go!"

Empty and possessed of considerable power, the T-4 was capable of eighty kilometers per hour. It accelerated down the lane, spewed gravel in every direction, and roared onto the highway. Baron's Hed lay to the east, a thirty-minute drive at most.

The highway had seen heavy use, but that was before the Imperials imposed a system of travel permits and "usage-" based taxes. In order to minimize costs and defend against bandits, farmers used heavily armed convoys to take their crops to market and rode tax-exempt farm animals for local transportation. Animal droppings lined the side of the road, which was otherwise clear.

What had been a convoy appeared up ahead, the line of burned-out hulks attesting not only to the dangers that lay in wait but the extent to which the Imperials allowed bandits to terrorize the land.

Kyle turned into a curve and felt the T-4 tilt in order to compensate. A turnout provided access to what had been a rest area. It was currently home to a band of Tusken Raiders. Though they were native to the planet Tatooine, the Tuskens had been brought in by the Imperials to function as "enforcers," a role they relished. The mercenaries had taken to the speeder bikes like an Aqualish to water and used them to "patrol" the local roads. None of them seemed to miss the bantha, the huge beasts they rode on Tatooine.

An advisory had gone out within seconds of Kyle's escape, and the Tuskens were prepared. Engines roared as they lurched into the air. Though vertical when parked, the long, sleek machines quickly went horizontal and formed on their leader, a Raider named Rogg.

Rogg knew his followers would be looking to him for encouragement. He waved a hand over his head and screamed a tribal war cry. It was lost in the slipstream. But it made him feel better.

The Tusken enjoyed his leadership position, liked the power it conveyed, but didn't relish moments like this. Rogg regarded the notion of leading from the front as impractical, especially since said leader eventually got killed, resulting in the loss of his valuable knowledge and experience, not to mention his life.

The Tusken leader had opened the matter for discussion, hoping the rest of the band would see how silly the traditional system was, but had been blocked by Bordo, his nominal number two, and one of two or three individuals who hoped to inherit his position.

Ah well, the charm pouch he wore around his neck had protected him this long and would again. The Tusken fired his dual-nose cannon and rejoiced as the coherent energy blipped toward the T-4's tailgate and blistered the transport's paint.

Kyle checked his mirror, saw the closely packed bikers, and spoke from the side of his mouth. "Take the controls, Weeg. I'll teach them some manners."

Wee Gee beeped by way of a response, activated the second set of controls, and wondered if he had the proper programming. A quick check revealed that the buttons, switches, and pedals arrayed before him weren't all that different from those on a combine, which was fortunate since Kyle had disappeared.

The turret gun sat in a lightly armored tub located behind the control cab. The agent climbed over the side, settled into the gunner's saddle, and flicked the power switch. An entire row of indicator lights flashed green.

Blaster bolts splashed on armor, flashed over the Rebel's head, and flew wide as the lead Tuskens fired their weapons.

Kyle found the safety, switched to "live fire," and peered through the sight. Though swerving back and forth in an attempt to ruin his aim, the bikers still formed a highly concentrated target. The firing studs were located to either end of the handlebar controls. The Rebel pressed with both thumbs, watched coherent light stutter into the tightly packed formation, and whooped when a bike exploded.

Debris flew in every direction and sliced off a biker's head, leaving the body intact. The torso was still in place, still gripping the controls when the two-wheeler smashed into a bridge support. The pieces went everywhere, narrowly missed the end of the formation, and threw up clouds of dirt.

The twenty-kilometer bridge led into Baron's Hed. Six lanes narrowed to four as Wee Gee guided the transport onto the span. He glanced into a side mirror, saw that the Tuskens were gaining, and pushed with his power grasper. Nothing happened. The droid realized that the accelerator was already on the floor.

Rogg had survived. The knowledge made him happy. He raised his right hand, gave a signal, and veered to the right. Kyle tracked the movement with the handlebar, fired a three-bolt burst, and swore when another rider was snatched from his seat. The bike swerved, narrowly avoided another, and tumbled end over end.

If Kyle was disappointed that Rogg survived, it was nothing compared to what Bordo felt. He was number two and had been for three long years. Three years of "Yes, Rogg, whatever you say, Rogg, and thank you, Rogg." It was enough to gag a Krayt dragon.

So Bordo led the second echelon over the left side of the transport, set his controls to auto, and dropped to the back.

He lost his balance, fell, and stood. A quick check was sufficient to make certain that the human was occupied by the need to repel additional boarders. Bordo staggered toward the opposite side of the transport. A single look confirmed that his cowardly leader had taken his own sweet time getting into position. Bordo smiled behind his bandages, waited for Rogg to look in his direction, and shot him in the goggles.

The speeder bike wobbled, veered away, and soared over the canyon. The engine quit, and the bike fell like a rock. Confident that his actions had been lost in the confusion of battle, Bordo waved the band ahead, turned in the direction of the control cab, and made his way forward.

Wee Gee saw an unrecognizable blob up ahead, zoomed in on it, and knew what it was. A roadblock! A *big* roadblock, capable of stopping the T-4 dead in its tracks. . . . He called for Kyle, knew the human couldn't hear, and wondered what to do.

Jan brought the *Moldy Crow* down from five thousand meters, found the ribbon of highway, and followed it toward the bridge. It had been difficult to watch over Kyle without being spotted, but she had managed to do so. Now, with the transport fleeing toward town and the bikers in hot pursuit, there was no need for pretense. If even one TIE fighter arrived — and was allowed to attack — the battle would be over. "*Crow* to Kyle — do you copy?"

Kyle had inserted the comm plug into his ear so long ago he had forgotten it was there. A Tusken had come aboard and was headed his way. The agent pulled his blaster. "Yeah, I copy — what took so long?"

"You told me to stay clear — remember?"

Kyle raised his weapon and watched the Tusken do likewise. "When did you start taking orders from me?"

"I don't," Jan said primly, "as you can tell from the fact that the *Crow* is hanging over your mostly empty head."

"Right," Kyle replied as he shot Bordo through the chest, "which brings us back to where we started. What took so long?"

Jan smiled and was about to reply when she noticed the roadblock. "They threw a barricade across the highway. Prepare for pickup."

Kyle saw the *Crow* start to descend and turned toward the cab. He threw himself forward. "Hey, Weeg! Set the controls to auto! Jan will pick us up!"

The droid didn't know who Jan was. But he had no desire to wind up as scrap. He did as he was told, rose from the passenger position, and turned toward the rear. A blaster bolt scored the side of his processor housing. He gave a long, drawn-out beep.

Kyle fired. A Tusken fell backward over the tailgate, was hit by one of the speeder bikes, and tumbled down the highway.

Wind whipped through Kyle's hair, and heat wrapped his shoulders as the *Crow* descended. The Tuskens fired at the ship as a hatch opened, a ramp was extended, and Jan shouted in Kyle's ear. "Here comes the roadblock! Jump!"

The Rebel heard her and was about to relay the order when he was snatched into the air. The droid had seen the ramp, grabbed the human's utility belt, and fired his repulsorlift engine. They had passed through the hatch by the time the transport hit the barricade.

The impact and the explosion that followed sent an AT-ST off the bridge, killed a platoon of stormtroopers, and created a wall of fire. Most of the surviving Tuskens were going too fast to stop. They screamed as their bikes raced into the conflagration and blew up.

A few, those blessed with quick reactions or positioned toward the rear of the pack, curved away. Heavy, dark smoke boiled up into the sky, pointed a finger toward the ship named *Vengeance*, and was blown away.

CHAPTER 6

Kyle squirmed forward, waited for Jan to join him, and looked down on Baron's Hed. It had been an attractive city once, back during his childhood, but things had changed since then. He brought the electrobinoculars up to his eyes, made a minor adjustment, and scanned the sprawl below.

A castlelike structure served as the natural focal point of the city. It was called Government House and stood at the very top of a hill called Baron's Knoll, the geological feature around which the town was built.

Though not as high as the hill on which the agents lay, the tower was tall enough to offer a tactical advantage to anyone who sought to defend it. It also forced those below to look up as if to a higher authority — a psychological trick that was anything but accidental. No less an entity than Jerec himself had supervised its construction during his brief tenure as Governor.

The city fell away from the stone-built house in a series of steps, not unlike a traditional wedding cake, with the wealthiest citizens living toward the top and the poor at the very bottom.

Walls that Kyle remembered as eye-catchingly white had been allowed to turn gray, almost black, and the gardens, traditionally red with pyro flowers at that time of year, were largely untended now, or home to the weapons emplacements, antenna farms, and other military equipment deployed to cope with Rebel attacks. Attacks that had increased since the day Morgan Katarn's head appeared on a spike.

The spaceport was located a half-klick to the east and showed signs of regular use. Repulsors flared as a freighter lifted off, paused as if to get its bearings, and departed toward the south.

"So," Jan said, allowing her glasses to fall, "What do you think?"

"I think it'll be tough," Kyle replied honestly. "The city is crawling with Imperial troops, bounty hunters, and mercenaries."

"Government House seems like the logical objective."

"Yeah, but how to get in? Knock on the door?"

"I could drop you on the roof."

"Thanks, but no thanks," Kyle replied. "You'd have to wait, and that would give them time to organize. Look at those weapons emplacements. They'd cut you to pieces."

Jan raised an eyebrow. "Me? Or the *Moldy Crow*?" She made it sound like a joke, but she knew it wasn't.

Kyle met her eyes and looked away. "*You*. The *Crow* can be replaced."

It was the closest the agent had come to declaring his feelings for her, and although Jan regretted the manner in which the comment had been elicited, she liked the response. The silence felt awkward. She broke it. "Be careful down there — call, and I'll come running."

Kyle smiled and indicated the comm unit on his wrist. "Don't worry. I will."

Jan nodded. She wanted to say something more but wasn't sure how it would come out. "Okay — see you later."

"Yeah," Kyle replied, swallowing the lump in his throat. "Later."

The female agent backed away, leaving Kyle to contemplate the city below. The sun had dropped toward the west, and lights twinkled through the evening haze. The city *looked* inviting, especially in the twilight, but Kyle knew better. He sighed and worked his way down off the skyline. A trail led toward the bottom. Gravity pulled him down.

The room was large but lacked external windows and felt dreary. A table had been placed at the center of the space and was bathed in light. 8t88 moved slightly, which caused the arm to do likewise. It was new, to him anyway, and had been removed from another 88 unit which he maintained for parts. How that machine felt or would manage without one of its limbs was of no interest to the droid. The arm had been flown in earlier that day. Lacking the services of a qualified roboticist, the droid had installed the part himself.

The wiring harness had been connected as had the tubes that carried hydraulic fluid to that particular extremity. He would fine-tune the wrist relay, adjust the roto-actuators, and test it out. Once that was accomplished, he would deal with the issue of the room.

8t88 held out his left hand. "Tuning stylus." The droid maintained a large retinue of servants, all of which were biologicals. The fact that "naturals" had created him and that he had enslaved them pleased the machine. Metal rang on metal as a human placed a tool in 88's hand. The droid threw it across the room. The *tuning stylus*, idiot! "Here — give me that."

The robot took the correct instrument, made the necessary adjustments, and was finished a short time later. "There," 8t88 said while making a fist, "that's better, *much* better. Summon the fool in charge."

8t88's henchmen, two humans and a Gamorrean, looked at each other, shrugged, and wrote off the request as one of the droid's numerous eccentricities. A human named Rol, the same one who couldn't tell the difference between a tuning stylus and a testing probe, left the room.

The person he sought — a rather snooty specimen who bragged that he had served Jerec during that individual's stint as planetary governor and for every executive since — had assumed what could only be described as airs. He took his own sweet time answering his page, preceded Rol up the stairs, and swept into the droid's somewhat Spartan quarters. The tiniest of smiles touched the majordomo's carefully pursed lips as he entered the room and bowed to 8t88. "Greetings, your eminence. Can I be of service?" The words dripped with condescension. They made even Rol uneasy.

"You can tell me about the history of this house," 8t88 replied smoothly.

"Why, certainly," the majordomo replied. "What would you like to know?"

"Let's start with this room," the droid said casually, waving toward his surroundings. "I notice it adjoins the ballroom. A rather unusual location for guest quarters. Tell me to what purpose this magnificent enclosure was originally dedicated — and why I was chosen to occupy it."

The majordomo swallowed nervously. The assignment had been a jest, his way of putting an uppity machine in its place while impressing the staff. The possibility that the droid could and would take him to task for it had never occurred to the increasingly nervous human. Tiny beads of perspiration appeared on his forehead. His hands started to shake. Should he apologize — or bluff it out? He chose the second, less humiliating alternative.

"This is a VIP suite, sire, chosen because of your stature and rank. And located in close proximity to your work."

8t88 wiggled his right index finger. It operated flawlessly, which pleased him. "Come a little closer, please. My amplifiers aren't what they used to be."

Rol exchanged looks with the Gamorrean. They knew that 8t88 could hear a pin drop from a hundred meters away.

Convinced that his story had been accepted, and eager to insinuate himself into the machine's good graces, the majordomo shuffled forward. He wore an elaborate, self-invented uniform. A robe dragged behind him. It was dirty where the edge touched the floor.

8t88 waited until the human was within range of his new right arm, reached out, and grabbed a fistful of robe. The majordomo's head snapped forward as the droid pulled him closer. "Look into my face — it's the last thing you will ever see."

The previously haughty servant seemed to come apart as he gazed into the machine's metal countenance. "Please! I'm sorry I gave offense — tell me how to make amends!"

"Ah," 88 said judiciously, "if only you could. But the malfunction is hidden within your skull, a difficult place to make repairs. I don't know if you've seen any brains lately, but they're hard to sort out. A CPU makes more sense."

The human was beside himself by now. A puddle had collected at his feet, and the guards wrinkled their noses — except for the Gamorrean, that is, who didn't notice. "My brain?"

"Why, yes," the droid replied. "Assuming you have one. . . . You know, the organ that believes it's superior to machines, and enjoys making fun of them."

The majordomo tried to object, tried to explain as the metal-cold hand spanned his face but soon lost interest. It seemed that the pressure, plus the sound of cracking facial bones, had caused him to faint. Not before he screamed, though — and sent birds fluttering out from the eaves.

>─┤─◆>─O─<◆─┤─<

If the security in and around Baron's Hed had been lacking before, it certainly wasn't now. Kyle's presence at the farm and subsequent escape had resulted in a heightened level of security.

Lines had formed in front of the city gates. Residents were eye-scanned prior to admission, and nonresidents were subject to interrogation. It was not a process the agent wanted to endure, especially given his status as a renegade and the price on his head. No, there had to be a better way to gain access, or so he hoped.

An hour passed while Kyle lurked in a heavily shadowed doorway and watched the western gate. Disguises, ruses, and all manner of clever and not-so-clever stratagems were conceived, considered, and rejected, including a potentially suicidal plan that involved climbing the wall and shooting the guards. There were so many plans, in fact, that he nearly failed to recognize the chance when it came.

The Imperials sent patrols out into the countryside on a regular basis, which meant that they returned at all hours of day and night. A pair of commandos on speeder bikes passed the doorway, followed by an armored hoverscout loaded with stormtroopers.

Kyle had been on similar patrols and knew how tiring they were. The troopers wanted to shuck their armor, take a shower, and find some beer. Their morale, like their state of readiness, was at its lowest ebb. . . . Perfect for someone as desperate as he was.

An AT-ST followed behind the hoverscout, and it — plus an unexpected diversion — provided the opportunity for which the Rebel had been waiting.

The diversion came courtesy of an unfortunate citizen who had the monumentally bad luck to drive his flock out into the arterial at the exact moment that the patrol happened past.

The speeder bikes sliced the herd in half, the gra ran in circles, and their owner tried to put things right. It wasn't easy, though, and the commandos didn't help when they kicked the goatlike animals, starting a panic.

What with the owner shouting, the gra bawling, and the Imperials swearing, Kyle had little difficulty slipping out of the doorway, dashing across a section of pavement, and jumping onto one of the AT-ST's podlike feet. Then, having plastered himself against the inside of the walker's leg, Kyle did his best to hang on, a seemingly simple task that turned out to be a good deal more difficult than he had predicted.

Riding the pod up off the heat-fused pavement was relatively simple. The hard part followed. The quarter-ton foot fell with alarming speed and struck the ground with so much force that Kyle nearly lost his grip. The impact made the agent's knees bend, sent a jolt up his spine, and rattled his teeth.

The whole thing was *so* bad that he barely noticed as the machine crushed a gra, minced through the remains of the herd, and turned toward a heavily guarded gate.

The agent held his breath as the sentry aimed a salute at the AT-ST's commanding officer, looked up when he should've looked down, and missed seeing a suspicious pair of arms.

Kyle held on for dear life as the machine made its way through

the warren of streets that comprised low town, the section of Baron's Hed where the poorest citizens lived and the majority of businesses were located.

The patrol turned a corner preparatory to heading for their barracks. The Rebel waited for a likely looking shadow, jumped just before the pod hit ground, and scurried for cover.

The agent hid in the shelter of a vine-draped wall, made sure that his departure had gone unnoticed, and straightened his clothes. The fact that they still bore traces of mud and grease would work in his favor. The idea was to fit in, and the citizens of low town weren't known for their sartorial splendor.

Kyle stepped out onto the street, adopted the air of someone who belonged there, and made for the center of town. The homes of high town were well lit, which gave definition to the hill on which they sat. Government House, which blazed with lights, crowned the very top. Finding it would be easy — getting in would be more difficult.

The side street gave way to Rimmer's Alley, a long, garishly lit thoroughfare that led to the base of the hill. Signs glowed, lights pulsed, and music blared beyond eternally open doors. The alleys stank of urine, vomit, and the incense used to cover up the smell.

Traffic, most of which was pedestrian, increased, and so did the danger. Kyle allowed his hand to drift toward his weapon as a brace of stormtroopers appeared on the far side of the street, paused to question a street vendor, and continued on their way. The agent felt relieved but knew the most dangerous adversaries would be less obvious.

A spacer lurched out of a bar, staggered to the curb, and threw up.

A droid, its extremities twisted by accident or design, begged for alms.

A woman, her makeup glowing as if lit from within, smiled and winked.

None posed a threat, but those hidden among them did. The Rodian bounty hunter, his eyes scanning for prey, the informer listening while he swept the street, and the Imperial agent made obvious by his boots — all were enemies.

Kyle walked the length of the street as quickly as he could without drawing undue attention to himself. It wasn't until he had left the main drag and entered the relative darkness of a residential area that the Rebel knew he'd been followed. He *felt* the other person's presence before he actually saw her with his eyes. The Force rippled away from the tail in the same manner that oil separates itself from water.

Kyle waited for the pool of light offered by one of the widely spaced streetlamps, paused as if looking for a landmark, and turned.

The tail made no attempt to mask her interest and nodded politely. The woman had been attractive once, but that was before her left eye had been destroyed and a bionic implant installed in its place. The device was equipped with a three-lens turret which whirred as it turned and delivered a tight shot to her hard-wired brain. Kyle noticed that the woman wore two blasters to his one. A sphere hovered over one shoulder, its purpose unclear. Her voice was deep and husky. "You looking for something, citizen? Maybe I can help."

"Thanks," Kyle replied, "but no thanks. How 'bout you? Would you like some directions? Or do you plan to follow me all night?"

"That's an interesting weapon you have there," the woman replied easily. "Kinda rare isn't it?"

Kyle cursed his own stupidity. The lightsaber was not only rare but valuable and certain to attract attention. He should have concealed it. The woman might or might not have help. Kyle had no desire to find out; he'd have to deal with her, and quickly.

"Yeah, it is kinda rare, sort of like that sphere over your shoulder. . . . Interested in a trade?"

Kyle moved his left hand toward the lightsaber and went for the blaster with his right. He pulled the weapon and fired it a tenth of a second before the would-be thief fired hers. Her bolt went wide — his struck her throat. She made a gargling sound and collapsed in a heap.

Kyle shifted his attention to the sphere, saw an eight-centimeter-long spike emerge, and backed away. The ball hummed menacingly, wove back and forth, and bored inward.

The agent backpedaled again, tried to correct his aim, and tripped on the curb. He fell over backward, felt the blaster fly out of his hand, and heard it clatter on the pavement. He was about to roll in that direction, about to expose his back to the needle-sharp probe, when a voice entered his mind. He'd heard it before — and knew it belonged to Rahn.

"Remember Nar Shaddaa? Go to the peace within."

Kyle remembered the landing platform, the manner in which time had slowed, and the ensuing battle. Achieving the necessary state was easier this time. The sphere slowed, and the hum became a low-pitched growl.

"Now," Rahn continued, "fight like a Jedi."

Kyle stood, thumbed a button, and heard the air crackle as the lightsaber came to life. Though slower now, the sphere continued its hypnotic motion.

"Good," Rahn said. "Now, close your eyes."

Kyle eyed the deadly looking sphere and shook his head. "I don't think that's a very good idea."

"Close your eyes, or I will leave. There are other students, some of whom show considerable promise." The criticism hurt, but the fact that Rahn regarded him as a student made Kyle feel good. He remembered the Academy's fencing instructor — a man who had expected unquestioning obedience from his students and never abused their trust. He closed his eyes.

"Now," Rahn continued, "*feel* the sphere, *feel* the way it moves, and merge with it."

Kyle tried to see himself the way the sphere would, as a heat signature, moving, but in ways that his on-board computer could analyze and extrapolate from.

"Excellent," Rahn said encouragingly. "You know where the sphere will go next. Aim for that spot."

Kyle "knew" the sphere would move to the right, brought the lightsaber down through the spot where it would be, and knew he'd missed.

"You were close," Rahn said, "*very* close. Try again."

Kyle tried again. He visualized a grid this time, green, with white lines, and "saw" the sphere displayed on it. It moved left, right, and left again. He sensed where the target would go and acted accordingly. As the agent opened his eyes, it was to confirm what he already knew. . . .

The sphere exploded, and a tiny fragment of hot plastic hit his cheek. Shrapnel flew, and time returned to normal. It felt as if an hour had passed, but a quick check of his chrono suggested otherwise. The entire incident had lasted no more than three or four minutes.

The Rebel hit the thumb switch, stuck the lightsaber through his belt, and retrieved his blaster. Time was passing — and there was reason to hurry.

Jerec couldn't see 8t88 in spite of the fact that the holographic projection was eight meters tall and more than eleven meters wide. He pretended that he could, though, knowing his actions would feed the carefully fashioned myths that surrounded him. Myths that overstated his considerable power by a factor of ten.

Still, he could *imagine* how 8t88 looked, along with the re-created mosaic and the holo-animated star map. Imagine, and glory in the knowledge that he was about to become the most powerful individual in the civilized worlds — no, in the *universe* — a position for which he was eminently suited.

"Well done, 8t88. The Valley of the Jedi will soon be mine. Meet the cargo ship *Sulon Star* at the refueling station outside of Baron's Hed. Your payment awaits."

The droid bobbed his head in what could have been interpreted as a nod or a bow, touched a button, and was gone.

Jerec turned his back to the holo tank and let the bridge crew gaze into long-dead eyes. Sariss was there — he could *feel* her presence. "We have what we came for. . . . Sariss, prepare the *Vengeance* for hyperspace."

Sariss bowed. "Yes, my lord."

Orders were given, drives engaged, and the ship broke orbit.

> ↦ ⊷ O ⊶ ↤

Though not possessed of the emotional nuances that human beings claim to experience, 8t88 felt what he imagined to be an enormous sense of satisfaction.

In order to complete his assignment, the droid had created a three-dimensional star map from the ceiling mosaic and beamed the digitized information up to the *Vengeance*. The original, which 8t88 continued to project toward the center of the room, floated before him. It was a thing of beauty. . . . He took one last look before shutting the image down. The map had been delivered, payment was assured, and he could afford to gloat.

The majordomo's death had worked wonders on the household staff, who had a sudden and unprecedented respect for intelligent machines. The thronelike chair was a little over the top, perhaps, but the symbolism was appreciated, and 8t88 took pleasure in using it. His pet, a winged monstrosity with an underthrust jaw and heavily lidded eyes, growled and crouched to his right. Its short, stubby tail made a thumping sound as it struck the wooden floor.

A long, ornately carved table stretched toward the far end of the room. Chairs stood to either side, some pulled back to allow access, some pushed forward. The reassembled mosaic occupied most of the table's surface. The beast growled and sniffed the air. The droid patted the monster's head. "What's the matter, my pet? Hungry again?"

The shadows stirred. Kyle Katarn stepped out into the light. He held a blaster in his hand. The beast rose to its feet. Saliva dripped from its jaws, and a growl rumbled deep in its throat. 88 took a grip on the animal's harness. "Not yet, my pet — you can eat him later."

"I see you found a new arm," Kyle commented lightly. "I should have aimed for your head."

The droid stood. An electronic signal went out. "Rol! Hontho! Trox! Take him!"

The Rebel shook his head mockingly. "Sorry, old rust bucket, but Rol and his friends are permanently indisposed. I want the map."

The droid gestured toward the table. "So? Take the map. Go ahead — put it in your pockets."

"Thanks," Kyle said dryly, "but no thanks. The digital version will be a good deal more convenient."

A motor whined, a section of ceiling started to descend, and light leaked around it. Kyle shifted his aim to cover the platform as a pair of legs appeared. 88 backed away. His pet resisted and left claw marks on floor.

Yun smiled, dropped to the table, and thumbed his lightsaber. It popped to life. "You want the map? Here, I'll cut it to size."

The lightsaber rose and fell. Super-heated tiles exploded. Kyle adjusted his aim and felt a sledgehammer hit his chest. Not a *real* sledgehammer but one shaped from the Force, and just as effective. He backpedaled and slammed into a chair. The blaster tumbled away, and Yun shook his head.

"So, this is what the light side sends against us. No wonder we succeed." So saying, lightsaber buzzing in his hand, he strode the length of the table. Broken tile skittered away from his boots.

Kyle recognized the Jedi as one of the three he'd seen at the farm . . . the young one.

The Rebel raised his feet, kicked the table, and did a backward somersault. The chair crashed to floor, and the agent landed on his knees.

8t88 dragged his still-unwilling pet into an alcove. A durasteel door slammed down in front of him. Machinery whined as the turbo-lift carried him upward.

Surprised by Kyle's move and more than a little intrigued, Yun moved forward. Kyle, who was still on his knees and at a disadvantage, pulled his lightsaber. Energy crackled and the smell of ozone filled the air as the Rebel managed to raise his weapon and block the Jedi's blow.

Yun frowned. It seemed that his opponent was more capable than the first impression would have suggested. The Jedi felt the tiniest trickle of fear enter his belly.

Kyle sensed the other man's hesitation, gained his feet, and allowed his opponent to disengage. In spite of the fact that his fencing lessons had made use of a fixed blade and his duel with the sphere had been somewhat brief, the combination gave the Rebel experience from which to draw. He concentrated on the Jedi's eyes, *felt* the Force flow around him, and lunged to the right.

Yun saw his adversary shift position, moved to intercept, and ducked as lethal energy swept through the space where his head had been. It was close. Too close for a complete novice.

Kyle struck again. Though slightly off, his blow sliced through the upper part of Yun's arm and drew blood, which was cauterized by the weapon's heat.

A cry escaped the Jedi's lips as the lightsaber fell from his hand, and he lost his balance and skidded on his back. Kyle approached, and Yun raised his arm. He was frightened, *very* frightened, but determined to maintain his pride. "So, kill me, Rebel, just as I would kill you!"

It seemed like good advice, and Kyle raised his weapon. But as he was about to strike, the other man's words echoed in his head. "Just as I would kill you." Was that the kind of man he wanted to be? The kind who would kill without reason? 8t88 had the map, and the Jedi had been neutralized. Kyle took three steps backward, lowered his weapon, and turned the device off. Rahn, absent till now, reappeared.

"Your father and I are proud of you, my son, for mercy is first and foremost among a Jedi's virtues."

Yun was amazed yet philosophical at the same time. There was something about the other Jedi's actions that *felt* right. But how could that be? Mercy was synonymous with weakness. He thought of Sariss, of how ashamed his mentor would be, and willed himself to be elsewhere. Yun floated toward the ceiling. His weapon followed.

Kyle watched for a moment, his eyes locked with Yun's, and realized his mistake. 8t88! The agent turned and raised his weapon. But the room was empty, or so it seemed until a blaster bolt sizzled past the agent's head. "There he is! Kill him!"

Blaster bolts flashed out of the darkness and bounced away as Kyle used the lightsaber to deflect them. The action seemed natural. But it threw a scare into the stormtroopers. "Did you see that? He's a Jedi!"

There was a pause as some of the troopers tried to run and were stopped by a blaster-wielding noncom. It was necessary to kneecap one of them before the tide turned.

Kyle retrieved his blaster, backed his way into a stairwell, and brought the wrist comm to his mouth. "Hey, Jan, how 'bout a lift?"

Jan circled the house, waited for an Imperial shuttle to clear the roof pad, and came in for a landing. "Ready and waiting, Kyle — meet me on the roof."

"Glad to hear it," Kyle replied, spraying the ballroom with blaster fire. "I seem to have overstayed my welcome."

"You have that effect on people sometimes," Jan agreed. "I'm the exception."

Kyle pounded up the stairs, pushed the door open, and stepped into the night. Repulsors flared as the *Crow* settled onto the pad. The agent grinned. "Lucky for me."

"Yeah," Jan agreed, "lucky for you. Now, get aboard."

Kyle ran up the ramp, entered the ship's belly, and made his way to the control room. "Did you see someone leave?"

"Yeah, a shuttle took off just as I came in."

Kyle swore. "That was 88. . . . The miserable pile of junk has the map! Don't let him escape!"

Jan knew she should have asked "What map?" but was tired of the charade. "No, sir. Yes, sir."

The *Crow* lifted free of the roof, turned as an anti-aircraft battery opened up, and blasted toward the south. A stream of energy bolts cut across the bow. Jan took evasive action. Kyle was thrown to the deck. He scrambled to his feet. "Thanks for the warning."

"Sorry. A slip of the hand, that's all. Better strap in."

Kyle did as he was told and watched Jan out of the corner of his eye. She was both wonderful and maddening at the same time. How did she manage that?

Lights appeared on the horizon, and Jan smiled.

CHAPTER 7

Fuel City had been sited ten klicks south of the spaceport for reasons of safety. It included rows of storage tanks, which were connected by a maze of pipes and served nine elevated refueling stations. Lights, which seemed to have been mounted helter-skelter throughout the complex, threw a thousand mysterious shadows.

The *Sulon Star* hovered by station six and was held in place by a network of interlocking tractor beams. Fuel entered the ship via hoses large enough to crawl through.

8t88 guided the shuttle in under the cargo vessel's belly and waited while computers communicated with each other. A hatch opened, and the shuttle rose inside a cone of greenish-blue light. The bay was intentionally small to maximize the vessel's cargo capacity. There were slots for four small craft, three of which were taken — two by lifeboats and one by an Imperial shuttle.

8t88 registered a sense of satisfaction as he engaged the ship's autopilot and left the cockpit. The shuttle belonged to the *Vengeance*. Jerec was efficient — a rare quality where biologicals were concerned, and one worth celebrating.

The beast licked himself, heard a noise, and turned in that direction. His tail thumped inquiringly. 88 nodded. "Yes, my pet, you can come."

The beast purred and stretched his wings while 88 released its harness. The machine would have preferred to leave the animal behind, but with no bodyguards to protect his back, the beast was better than nothing.

They left the shuttle, made their way to a hatch, and waited for it to open. There was no one to greet them — an insult the droid wouldn't forget, and still another manifestation of antimachine bias.

Footsteps echoed off bulkheads, and claws clicked on metal as the twosome made their way through empty corridors and entered the ship's wardroom. Light gleamed off the surface of a scratched metal table, shadows clung to recesses set into the bulkheads, and there were no signs of life. The droid's hip squeaked as he turned. "Hello? Anyone here?"

Something stirred. One, no, *two* figures separated themselves from the darkness and stepped out into the light. 8t88 felt the same sense of not-rightness that humans refer to when they have a "bad feeling" about something. Gorc? Pic? Why would Jerec dispatch Jedi on what amounted to a routine errand? Or had someone decided to afford him the respect he was due? Yes, the droid decided, that would explain it. He spoke with the authority natural to a superior being. "I'm here to collect my pay."

The "twins" smiled, but the expressions were empty of humor. It was Pic who spoke. "Good — because we're here to deliver it."

>—+—◆>—◦—<◆—+—<

Jan was still apologizing to Fuel City air control, still making excuses, as the *Crow* departed. "Sorry about that, Control. I got confused, that's all. Over."

Captain Zyak was well aware of how confused civilian pilots could be. He shook his head in disgust. He wore a pencil-thin mustache and a standard-issue sneer. "Copy, one-niner-two. Just get that pile of junk off my screen. And be more careful in the future."

Jan grinned. "Roger that, Control."

Zyak liked the sound of her voice and decided to offer some advice. "Watch your vector, one-niner-two, there was trouble in Baron's Hed, and it would be real easy for one of those missile batteries to make a mistake. Over."

Jan struggled to sound concerned. "Trouble — yes, sir — thanks for the tip. Over."

Zyak walked to the window and watched the running lights lose themselves among the galaxy of floods. He wondered what the pilot looked like and knew he would never get to find out. Life, if that's what this tour of duty could be called, was anything but fair.

>—+—◆>—◦—<◆—+—<

Kyle watched the *Crow* depart, waited long enough to ensure that Jan was okay, and turned to the task at hand. Tracking 8t88 was made more difficult by the fact that machines didn't seem to disturb the Force the way living beings did.

Thanks to the fact that only three of the nine refueling stations were occupied, however, the agent was able to narrow his choices. One vessel was too small, and one was fully automated, which left a cargo vessel named the *Sulon Star*. The Rebel chose what appeared to be the correct catwalk. It was empty and rang to his footsteps.

As with most vessels of her type, the *Sulon Star* was equipped with an emergency-access hatch located on the topmost surface of her hull. The catwalk passed approximately ten meters above it. Kyle paused, checked the surrounding area, and swung his legs over the railing. The jump seemed do-able, in spite of the hull's curvature.

Having checked his weapons to make sure they were secure, the agent stepped out into midair and fell like a rock. He absorbed most of the impact with bent knees, checked to make sure the jump was unobserved, and made his way to the hatch.

The top hatch, like the rest of the ship's locks, was open in compliance with the station's safety regs. The open ports would allow autohoses to enter in case of fire while the crew escaped.

Kyle had concocted a story to explain his presence should he run into a crew member. But he wasn't called upon to use it. The agent lowered himself through the lock and dropped into the corridor all without challenge.

Was the ship deserted? It seemed that way until Kyle *felt* the Force ripple away from something and knew others were about. 8t88? No, but the feeling was reminiscent of the droid's loathsome pet. And if the pet was present . . .

Cautious now, and having no desire to go head-to-head with the winged beast, Kyle pulled his blaster.

The corridor curved right, and he curved with it. He could *feel* the creature. And something less defined, as if it were somehow screened.

The agent rounded a corner, saw light spill out through a hatch, and paralleled the bulkhead. He paused next to the opening, listened for movement, and heard air whisper through the overhead ducting. It was strange, *very* strange, and Kyle didn't like it.

The Rebel narrowed his eyes, rewrapped his fingers around his blaster, and made his move. He slipped through the hatch, put a layer of durasteel behind his back, and scanned the compartment.

He saw 88 and heard the growl at the same moment. The droid was seated in a chair with his back to the door, and the monster squatted beyond. Its eyes were red and made tunnels through the darkness. Kyle half expected the beast to attack, but it remained where it was. Somewhat reassured but ready to fire if the need arose, the Rebel moved forward. "I've been waiting for this moment."

"And so have I," a voice said.

A number of things happened at once. 8t88's head toppled from his shoulders, bounced off his lap, and rolled across the deck. The monster pounced, swallowed the tidbit whole, and looked surprised.

Kyle heard the voice and turned toward the sound. A mental shield dropped, and the shadows produced something huge. It wore a helmet, chin guard, and chest armor. . . . But of even more importance was the enormous lightsaber that the Dark Jedi clutched in a three-fingered hand. The air crackled as the monstrous weapon scythed through the air.

Kyle frowned, wondered how a Jedi could be so stupid, and shot Gorc in the face. The giant swayed and toppled backward. He landed with a thud. His lightsaber pinwheeled through the air, hit handle-down, and turned itself off.

Kyle was still thinking about what had occurred when a banshee dropped onto his back and sank razor-sharp talons into his flesh. "You killed Gorc! Now *you* will pay!"

Kyle attempted to shake the assailant off, felt a blade nick the side of his throat, and released the blaster. Fingers sought the agent's eyes as he reached up and back. He found a bone-thin arm and wrestled with it as he backpedaled across the room. The agent hit the bulkhead as hard as he could. There was a crunching sound.

Pic uttered a high-pitched scream, directed a blast of energy at Kyle's mind, and fell to the deck.

Stunned by the attack and bleeding from a half-dozen puncture wounds, Kyle staggered away.

Aroused by the scent of blood and eager to make an easy kill, the beast launched its attack. The monster's claws made a scratching noise as they sought traction on the deck. A roar emanated from deep within its throat as it charged.

Though slowed by the pain in his head, Kyle still managed to pull the lightsaber from his belt and turn. The weapon blurred through the air, took the monster in the mouth, and cut off the top of its head.

Kyle was unaware that the animal was dead — its legs continued to pump — until the monster hit an equipment locker and collapsed. Metal buckled, doors popped open, and spare parts spilled onto the deck.

Dazed, and glad to be alive, Kyle killed the lightsaber and fell into a chair. The once-immaculate room had been transformed into a charnel house. The sight of it, not to mention the smell of it, made him nauseous.

Slowly, so as to minimize the pain, the agent rose to his feet. He stood over the monster and pondered what to do. The creature lay facedown, or would have, had its face survived.

The Rebel grabbed hold of a quickly stiffening leg, levered the monster over, and re-lit the lightsaber. The smell of burnt hair filled Kyle's nostrils as he made a long, only slightly wavy incision.

The agent gagged as coils of blue-green intestine boiled out of the monster's abdominal cavity and squirmed over the deck. There were three stomachs to choose from. But only one looked twice its normal size.

Wrinkling his nose in disgust, Kyle sliced the organ open, spotted 88's head, and reached in to get it. The agent's fingers slid through a coating of green bile, found the droid's scanner sockets, and used them to secure purchase. Kyle pulled the casing free and fought a series of dry heaves.

Having wiped the head dry with linen taken from a locker, the agent was about to depart when a high-pitched scream caused him to turn.

Pic had regained consciousness. The Jedi was little more than a blur. He had covered half the distance between them and was airborne by the time the Rebel started to react. There was no time to think. Instinct took over.

The head weighed a good ten kilos and was made of metal. It described an arc around Kyle's body and struck with considerable force. There was a loud cracking noise as skull hit skull, and Pic, who resembled nothing so much as a rag doll, flew across the compartment, smashed into a bulkhead, and fell to the deck.

Paranoid by now, the Rebel recovered his blaster, checked each body for a sign of life, and left the compartment. The safest, most expedient thing to do was to return the way he had come.

Kyle turned to the left, heard someone shout, and sensed rather than saw the energy bolt that flashed past his head. The agent yelled into his wrist comm and ducked around a corner. He had what he'd come for. But could he escape?

>─┼─◆>─○─<◆─┼─<

The 3-D print had been rolled into a cylinder and secured with a piece of wire. Jan had come across the item while searching for her multi-tool and had opened it up. A woman stared out at her, a woman so pretty that Jan felt momentarily jealous until she recognized Kyle's eyes and knew where they had come from. Here was a woman who had loved him, too, albeit in a different way.

The sound of his voice made her jump. "Hey, Jan. I got what I came for, but these clowns want it back. How 'bout a ride? Over."

Jan took her boots off the console and spoke into her headset. "Hang in there. I'm on my way. Over."

All the major systems were on-line. Jan flipped some switches, waited for the corresponding green lights, and fired the ship's repulsors. The *Crow* went straight up.

A farmer returning from a late-night errand saw the starship rise out of the hollow, lost control of his gravsled, and took a nasty tumble.

Jan turned the bow toward Fuel City and added power. The lighthearted banter didn't fool her for a moment — Kyle was in trouble. Seconds would count.

She was low this time — so low, that Fuel City Control wouldn't see her till it was too late. A flock of gra scattered as she skimmed a hilltop, and lights twinkled on the horizon.

It seemed as if someone had called for help because the ship was crawling with troops. Kyle shot an officer, hurtled down the passageway, and saw the access ladder.

Armored legs appeared, followed by a stormtrooper's torso. His boots hit the deck; he turned, saw Kyle, and went for his assault weapon. It was slung across his back and not readily accessible. The agent shot the Imperial three times in quick succession and watched him fall.

An indicator flashed red and signaled the need for a fresh power pack. There were backups on the agent's belt but no time to mess with them, not with a perfectly good assault rifle waiting to be taken. He holstered the blaster, grabbed the more powerful weapon, and spun toward the other end of the passageway.

A trio of Commandos came around the corner, paused by their officer's body, and opened fire.

Kyle ducked, fired three short bursts, and brought two of them down. The third thought better of the whole thing and fled.

Kyle took advantage of the respite to scramble up the ladder and slam the inner hatch. Two minutes' worth of sustained fire was sufficient to spot-weld the door in place.

Once that was accomplished, the Rebel climbed through the lock and stuck his head outside. There was no sign of Jan. But there was lots of opposition. Ten or twelve Imperials were visible on the catwalks around him. A trooper spotted him, yelled something incoherent, and opened fire.

Thankful for the protection offered by the lock, Kyle returned the favor. The Imperial threw out his arms and fell into the darkness below. Orders were shouted, and fire came from all around.

Captain Zyak had completed his shift and was about to head for his quarters when all heck broke loose. Information was hard to come by, but judging from fragmentary comm traffic and the manner in which energy beams zipped back and forth, a full-fledged firefight was under way.

Given the fact that his replacement — a sallow-faced specimen named Nomo — had just graduated from air-traffic control school, the officer decided to stay. He peered through electrobinoculars and spoke from the side of his mouth.

"Lieutenant Nomo. Get ahold of the idiot in charge of those troops and remind him that they named this complex 'Fuel City' for a reason. One shot in the wrong place and every single one of us is dead."

Nomo's hand shook as he lifted a comlink and made the necessary call.

"Incoming ship," a tech said laconically. "Vector eight — and coming fast."

"Tell them to break it off," Zyak ordered, scanning the battle below. "I have enough problems."

"I spoke with their commanding officer," Nomo said urgently. "He has orders to kill the infiltrators regardless of cost."

"His butt will be the first to fry," the officer said wearily, "but there's no reasoning with people like that. Call operations — tell them to stop the pumps and bleed the pipes. Order switching to close valves one through forty-six. The less fuel in circulation, the better."

"The incoming craft suggests that we perform an unnatural act on ourselves," the tech said patiently. "Response?"

Zyak turned, strode over to the tech's position, and scanned his screens. He'd seen the target before. One-niner-two was back — and there was very little doubt as to why. . . . The pilot with the nice voice had dropped a team of agents into *his* complex and was planning to extract them. Zyak remembered the advice he had given and felt betrayed. It was stupid — he knew that — but that's how he felt.

"Blow her out of the sky," Zyak said flatly, "and do it now."

Jan kicked the *Crow* from port to starboard in an effort to confuse the surface-to-air missile batteries. She heard a tone as the weapons were launched. The ship's computer found the missiles, classified them by type, and fed the information to her console.

Jan ejected chaff in an effort to create more targets, fired four antimissile missiles, and used her energy cannon to strafe an outlying fuel tank. It exploded, attracted every heat-seeking missile then in the air, and erupted again. An obscene red-orange flower blossomed, consuming everything around it, and sent petals toward the sky.

"By all the gods," Nomo said, his voice filled with wonder, "look at that! We blew the ship out of the air!"

"*That* was storage tank sixteen, you idiot," Zyak replied crossly. "Have they bled the pipes yet?"

Nomo checked a console. "Not entirely, sir. They read seventy percent and falling."

"And the valves?"

"They're working on it — some kind of relay went down. What's so important about bleeding the . . . "

Nomo's question was cut short as tanks fifteen, fourteen, and thirteen blew in quick succession. The explosions shook the transparisteel windows and sent a mug crashing to the deck. Fires, each overlapping the next, lit the night.

"That's why the pipes are so important," Zyak said bleakly. "As long as they have fuel in them and the valves remain open, they function as fuses. Well, Nomo, it's *your* shift. Sort this one out and you'll be a Captain by Monday. Fail, and you'll be working in the mines."

The color drained from the younger officer's face as he watched Zyak remove personal items from a drawer. "Mines? What mines? Where will you go?"

"As far as I can," Zyak said grimly. "As far as I can."

The *Crow* banked left, then right as Jan guided the ship between pillars of fire. The control tower appeared on the left, and she passed within fifty meters of it. A frightened face peered out and disappeared. "Kyle? Where the heck are you? We won't get a second chance. Over."

Kyle watched another storage tank explode off to the north, realized the destruction was marching his way, and spoke into his wrist comm. "Look for station six. I'm on the top surface of a large cargo ship. Over."

Fuel City's computerized docking system was still up and running. A diagram appeared on the *Crow*'s nav screen. Jan spotted station six, dodged a communications pylon, and fired her retros. The ship slowed, dropped into the appropriate approach slot, and eased forward. Blaster fire splashed against the ship's hull but lacked the force to penetrate. The larger, more powerful weapons, the ones assigned to defend the entire complex, were equipped with stops that prevented them from firing on a fueling station — a rather wise precaution, all things considered.

The *Crow* was backlit by a distant fire. Kyle raised his arms and brought his wrists together as the ship coasted into position. The ramp whirred, and jerked to a stop. A gust of wind hit the starboard side of the hull, and Jan fought for control.

The agent checked to make sure that he had a good grip on 88's head, waited for the ramp to swing his way, and made the necessary jump. The ramp bounced, swayed, and pulled Kyle up. Energy bolts flashed, but none came close enough to worry about.

Once inside, Kyle made his way to the cockpit. Jan wrinkled her nose. "Who's your friend? He could use some deodorant."

Kyle grinned. "Jan, meet 8t88. What's left of him, anyway. 8t88, meet Jan. She's cranky sometimes. But very good looking. Not something *you* could relate to."

It was a nice compliment, and one that Jan would have enjoyed a lot more if the circumstances had been different. Sensors went off as a TIE fighter approached. She performed a wing-over, circled a still-intact storage unit, and opened fire. The enemy ship seemed to stagger, nose-dived into the tank, and triggered a massive explosion. Shrapnel flew in every direction, punctured a line, and sent fuel spilling out onto the ground. A piece of still-burning debris splashed into the liquid and set it afire. The lake expanded and wrapped the maintenance facility in a red-hot embrace.

Kyle swallowed and fought the desire to grab the controls. "Where the heck did *he* come from?"

"I believe TIE fighters are manufactured by Sienar Fleet Systems," Jan replied sweetly, "or were you referring to the pilot?"

"Ex-pilot," Kyle said dryly. "Head for the Nefra Canyons. Maybe we can lose them."

Though not as familiar with Sulon as Kyle, Jan knew the canyons were part of the dry, semiarid region that lay just beyond the Hanto mountain range, only minutes away as the crow flies. The sun had broken over the eastern horizon by then and flooded the land with pink light.

Jan turned toward the east, saw Kyle rise from his chair, and knew what he intended to do. The *Crow* was vulnerable from behind.

Mountains appeared ahead. A brace of TIE fighters took up position behind them and opened fire. Jan jinked back and forth. The cannon fire went wide.

A pair of jagged peaks stabbed the sky. They were so close together that locals referred to them as "the twins." Jan spoke into a wire-thin boom mike. "Grab something solid — and hang tight."

The *Crow* stood on her right wing as she passed between the peaks. Kyle, who had opened the top hatch and was facing backward, had a bird's-eye view of what happened next.

The first TIE fighter imitated Jan's move and made it through the gap. The second wasn't so fortunate. It was hard to tell what went wrong, whether the pilot misjudged the distances involved or experienced a momentary malfunction. Whatever the reason, the Imperial ship caught the side of a peak, exploded, and sent an avalanche thundering toward the base of the mountain.

The surviving pilot hung back for a moment, seemed to regain his confidence, and took up the chase.

Kyle fought the backward pressure exerted by the slipstream and drew his blaster. It contained a fresh power pack, and the indicator glowed green. The agent struggled to hold the weapon steady, pressed the firing stud, and watched energy blip toward the fighter. It was really kind of silly, like hunting a krayt dragon with a peashooter, but something was better than nothing. The Imperial ignored Kyle and opened fire. The bolts went wide.

Jan eyed the labyrinth of canyons, wished she knew them better, and put the ship into a long, shallow dive.

Reddish-brown walls rose around the *Crow* as the agent dived into one of the larger ravines, followed it to the right, and passed beneath a land bridge.

Kyle watched heavily eroded cliffs flash by, hoped Jan knew what she was doing, and forced himself to let it go. The Rebel felt a tremendous sense of calm as everything seemed to slow. Now he had time to think — to concentrate. He fired, rode the burst of energy outward, and flew wide of the target.

The agent corrected his aim, "saw" where the TIE fighter would go next, and triggered the next shot. He rode this one all the way to the transparisteel canopy that protected the Imperial pilot and felt himself dissipate against it. Though not strong enough to punch its way through, the energy bolt did manage to blister the outer surface of the windshield.

The pilot leaned over sideways in an attempt to see around the blockage, lost his concentration, and paid for the mistake with his life.

Jan saw a cliff hurtling toward her face, pulled back on the control yoke, and felt something heavy hit the bottom of her stomach.

The *Crow* stood on her tail, Kyle struggled to hang on, and the TIE fighter kept going. It hit the wall, exploded, and showered the canyon with debris.

Jan leveled out, checked her sensors, and spoke into the mike. "Kyle? Are you okay?"

The voice came from right beside her as Kyle dropped into the co-pilot's seat. "No, I'm *not* okay — you took five years off my life."

Jan smiled. "And why not? I've saved it enough times. Where to?"

"The farm — so 88 can tell us what he knows."

"Does that make sense? Your father's place was crawling with Imperials."

Kyle nodded. "Yeah, but I'm guessing they're gone by now, pulled off to deal with the problems in Baron's Hed and Fuel City."

Jan looked toward the south. A column of smoke marked the spot where the refueling complex was located. And, judging from the way it billowed upward, the fires continued to burn. "You could be right. But how 'bout some sleep? Say, eight hours' worth?"

Kyle gave it some thought. A rest would feel good — and would give the Imperials that much more time to clear the farm. "Copy that . . . Sleep first, farm second."

>-+++-O-++-+-<

The sun hung low in the sky, shadows pointed toward the east, and the day was coming to an end. Jan circled the farm for the third time, searched the ground for signs of Imperial troops, and failed to see any. "Looks like you were right, Kyle. I'll put her down."

The agent nodded. Jan had hidden the *Crow* in the ruins of a long-defunct factory, where a section of partially intact roof screened the vessel from orbital scrutiny. Snug in their hiding place and with Wee Gee to serve as a lookout, they slept through most of the day.

They awoke well past noon and took turns in the fresher. Jan tended to Kyle's cuts, scratches, and puncture wounds, and he made dinner. They ate outside, sitting within the ruins of a once-prosperous factory, talking about simple things — things that had nothing to do with war, fear, and death. It felt good and left both of them re-energized.

>-+++-O-++-+-<

There was a gentle thump as the ship touched down. They left the vessel with blasters in hand. There were tracks but no sign of the troops who had made them. Kyle returned the blaster to its holster, called Wee Gee, and led the way to the house.

Hinges squeaked as the door swung open. Kyle checked for booby traps, failed to find any, and stepped inside. Things were just as he'd left them. Jan had never been in the house before and tried to imagine what it had been like — the man with the beard going about his work while a little boy took things apart and put them back together again — not unlike the many happy hours she had spent with *her* father. Kyle's voice brought her back to the present. "Jan? What are you smiling about?"

Caught unawares, and more than a little embarrassed, Jan shrugged. "Nothing special. So where's this workshop I've heard so much about?"

"Right this way," Kyle replied. "Watch your step, though — our guests forgot to clean up after themselves."

The lights came on, and after a little bit of searching, Kyle found the items he required. It took the better part of ten minutes to locate the necessary cables, make the proper connections, and hook the droids together. "There," Jan said, "that should do it. What now?"

"Now, we learn something very important," Kyle said gravely. "Something my father and at least one Jedi gave their lives to protect — the coordinates for a long-lost world and the Valley of the Jedi."

The way that he said it sent a tingle down Jan's spine. Wee Gee held the droid's head aloft and sent the necessary signal. Beams of light shot out of 88's eyes, and a series of seemingly random images appeared, followed by the one Kyle had been waiting for: a shot of the reconstructed ceiling mosaic, followed by layer after layer of star maps and a shot of an orange-green world.

Kyle gave a whoop of joy, and grabbed Jan and danced her around the room. She laughed and tripped on a pile of debris.

Kyle saved her from a fall, held her in his arms, and looked into her eyes. He liked what he saw there, and what he felt as their lips touched.

Finally, after what seemed like a long time but actually was not, the kiss came to an end. Kyle felt awkward and slightly embarrassed. "Sorry. I didn't mean to take advantage."

Jan shook her head. "Don't be. I'm not."

Repulsors rumbled, the walls shook, and Kyle went for his blaster. An extremely strong personality had arrived. One that sent waves through the Force and seemed to radiate strength. "The

Imperials! They're back! Disconnect the head. Come on, Weeg — let's get out of here."

The agent dashed out of the workshop and entered the living room. With a quick glance through the window, he skidded to a halt. A ship had landed, all right. But not the kind he had expected. The Rebel X-wing sat more than a hundred meters away. Its pilot, a man not that much older than Kyle himself, stood before the tap tree.

Something about the man's stance, the way in which he paused to pay his respects to another life form, was more eloquent than words. That plus the lightsaber that hung by his side signaled who and what he was: a Jedi Knight.

Jan spoke from beside him. "That's Luke Skywalker. I met him aboard the *New Hope*."

Kyle frowned. "Skywalker? Here? Why?"

"I think he was sent to check on us," Jan said gently, "to see how we're doing."

Suddenly, Kyle was bedridden again, watching through half-slit eyes as Jan placed something in one of his pockets. "You took the disk and gave it to them! They sent you to spy on me!"

His voice was filled with anger, and Jan hardened herself against it. "Yes, I did." The agent's chin came up, and her eyes glowed with defiance. "And I'd do it again. I love you, Kyle Katarn. But I love freedom even more. . . . The Valley of the Jedi is *too* important, *too* dangerous, for you to handle alone."

Kyle shook his head. "And to think that I trusted you."

Now it was Jan's turn to be angry. "Did you? Is that why you kept everything to yourself — asked me to risk my life for something I didn't know about — treated me like a convenience — ignored the chain of command — acted as if you were smarter than everyone else?"

They were harsh words made all the worse by the fact that Kyle knew they were true. One part of him wanted to strike back, to hurt Jan in the same way that she had hurt him, but another, wiser aspect of his personality offered counsel. Which was more important? His pride? Or the relationship his words could destroy?

Silence hung like a blanket between them. Jan waited. What would Kyle say? What would he do?

Finally, after what seemed like an eternity, he took her hands in his. "I'm sorry, Jan. It won't happen again."

Jan kissed Kyle on the cheek, took him by the hand, and led him outside. Skywalker, who seemed to have been waiting for such a move, turned in their direction. He smiled and held out his hand. "Kyle Katarn — Luke Skywalker. It's a pleasure to meet you."

Kyle blushed at the unexpected compliment. "Thanks. The pleasure is mutual."

Skywalker gestured toward the lightsaber thrust through Kyle's belt. "That comes with a price, you know."

Kyle shrugged. "Everything does."

"You found the coordinates?"

Kyle nodded. "Yes, but Jerec got to them first."

The other Jedi looked thoughtful. "You plan to go there?"

Kyle looked at Jan, saw her nod, and looked back. "Somebody has to."

Skywalker was silent for a moment — as if listening to someone they couldn't see or hear. The words he spoke raised goose bumps on Kyle Katarn's arms. "Yes — for it is written that 'a Knight shall come, a battle will be fought, and the prisoners go free.'"

Jan was the first to break the ensuing silence. "Those words — where did they come from?"

Skywalker smiled. "I'm not sure. But *I* heard them from a Jedi who never was — a soldier who gave his life for freedom — and a father who believed in his son. . . . A man named Morgan Katarn."

The tap tree didn't notice when the Rebels left. True to its nature, it danced with the wind, took communion from the stars, and pulled sustenance through its roots. For the tap tree, like all its kind, knew the sun would return.

DATE DUE

MAR 02 2001		
MAR 15 2001		

DEMCO 13829810